The Daring Duke

(THE 1797 CLUB BOOK 1)

By

*USA Today Bestseller
Jess Michaels*

THE DARING DUKE
The 1797 Club Book 1
1797Club.com

For more information, contact Jess Michaels
www.AuthorJessMichaels.com

To contact the author:
Email: Jess@AuthorJessMichaels.com
Twitter www.twitter.com/JessMichaelsbks
Facebook: www.facebook.com/JessMichaelsBks

Jess Michaels raffles a FREE Kindle or Amazon gift certificate EVERY month to members of her newsletter, so sign up on her website: http://www.authorjessmichaels.com/

DEDICATION

To my Mom, who wanted me to say that she is neither a grasping social climber nor a drunk. She does help me with copyedits and is one of my biggest fans, which makes writing that much more fun. Love you Mom!

And to Michael. Twenty years of marriage and you're still my best friend and the person I want to share all my moments with. Thank you for being my everything.

AUTHOR'S NOTE:

When I had the idea for the 1797 Club series in February of 2016, it started off as a bit of a joke between historical romance writer friends. "Why not a series of ALL DUKES?" we joked around during a conference.

By the time the weekend was over, I had rough plotted out a series concept. Now over the last year that has developed quite a bit, but I'm so pleased to present to you this ten-book series about a group of friends who vow to help each other as they each inherit one of the highest titles in the land. I have fallen in love with these men, these brothers in spirit, and I hope you'll love each and every one of them and their feisty and fierce heroines, as well.

Enjoy!

P.S. – Join the Club! www.1797club.com

PROLOGUE

Spring 1797

James Rylon stiffened as he watched his father stride across the lawn at Braxton Academy toward him and his two best friends. His heart began to race, he felt the blood drain from his face. The once monthly visits from the Duke of Abernathe were something he dreaded immensely.

"He always looks so cross," James's best friend Graham muttered.

James swallowed, trying hard not to allow his fear to enter his face. At fourteen, he didn't like showing that kind of weakness, even to his best friends. "He *is* always cross," he whispered.

His other best friend, Simon, shook his head. "Makes me appreciate my own father a bit more. He mostly just ignores me."

James bit his tongue, unwilling to say what was on his mind. Unwilling to let a crack enter his voice when he admitted that his own father despised him.

The Duke of Abernathe reached them at last and scowled at his son. "Pulham."

James flinched. Since he was ten, his father had insisted on calling him by his courtesy title. But he wasn't the Earl of

Pulham. He was James. His sister called him James. When his mother was sober enough to be awake, she called him James. All his friends and teachers called him James.

The title felt like a yoke his father put around his neck. A weight he could hardly bear with his skinny body.

"Father," he responded.

His father reared back and slapped James across the face hard enough that for a moment James saw stars before his eyes. He couldn't hold back a humiliating gasp of pain as he jerked his hand up to cover his stinging cheek.

"You shall call me Your Grace or Abernathe, or at minimum, sir." His father shook his head. "You are *far* too old for this Father nonsense."

James jerked out a nod. "Y-yes, Your Grace."

The duke quickly glanced at his friends, and James did the same. Simon had turned his face and was staring intently at a spot far off in the distance. Graham, on the other hand, was standing ramrod straight, hands fisted at his sides, glaring at James's father. And being the only one who had begun to grow into a man's body, it was a rather intimidating sight.

But Abernathe only chuckled at the challenge in the other boy's stare. "Mind yourself, boy. You're not a duke yet." He turned his attention back to his son. "Come, Pulham. Walk with me."

James swallowed past the lump in his throat and did so, stepping into line beside his father as they took their monthly turn around the garden behind Braxton Academy. As always, his father did not ask after him or his studies. He simply barked out questions, ones about the House of Lords, ones about managing estates, ones about title. And, as usual, James stammered answers, most of them wrong, while his father screamed and threatened.

When the customary quarter of an hour visit was over, Abernathe stopped in his tracks and turned to look down at James.

"You are hopeless," his father said with a shake of his head.

"Not all my sons were failures. A shame the one who will take my title is. Good day, Pulham."

He turned on his heel then and walked away without so much as a backward glance. James stared after him, his chest brewing with a combination of rage and heartache and guilt. Tears stung his eyes and he bent at the waist, breathing shallowly as he tried to fight them. Fight the weakness. Make it go away.

The bell at the door was being rung, signaling the time had come to cease in sport and exercise and return to classes. James let out a pained grunt. He had to go back. He'd have to face all the others in his classes, his teachers. They would see this weakness. The one he usually hid with good humor and playfulness.

The weakness that rotted him out from the inside where no one could see.

"James?"

He tensed, straightening at the mention of his name. He turned to find Simon and Graham standing a few feet away. He wiped at his eyes, heat filling his cheeks that they'd seen him in such a state.

"What?" he barked, much louder and more urgently than he should have.

Simon stared at him a long moment, then came up and slung an arm around James's shoulder. "Come on. Let's sneak off to the creek."

Graham's face lit up. "Oh yes, let's do! I don't want to go listen to Old Comey drone on and on about figures for the next hour and a half. I'd much rather fish."

James nodded. "All right."

They began to walk away from the school, through the garden, over a low spot in the wall that enclosed it and out into the countryside that surrounded Braxton Academy. They had been walking for over five minutes before anyone spoke.

"Why is he so cruel to you?" Graham asked.

Humiliation flowed through him. He'd spent a lifetime having his father harangue him in front of others, but never in

3

front of Graham and Simon. He liked both boys—they had become fast friends, along with a group of others, since he began at Braxton Academy the previous year. He had thrived at the Academy, out from under his father's shadow, out of his house where he felt so unwanted and unloved.

"No one else saw or heard him," Graham assured him. "Simon and I simply followed. I was worried."

"Worried about what?" James whispered.

"That he might strike you again," Graham said, this time through clenched teeth.

Simon shot their friend a look before he said, "James, what did he mean when he said not all his sons were failures? You don't have any brothers, do you?"

James took a long breath as they crested a low hill and reached the creek at the outer edge of the school property. As Graham dug behind a tree for the fishing poles hidden there, James pondered his response.

He had never felt safe to discuss his family dynamics. They were complicated and ugly. But with these two boys, he knew he could be more open. And at the moment he was too exhausted to be anything but.

He sat down on the creek's edge and stared at the bubbling water as he said, "I *did* have an older brother, older by fifteen years. A half-brother, Leonard. I never met him, though. He died before I was born. That's why my father married my mother at all, to produce another heir."

Simon stared at him. "How did he die?"

"An accident," James said with a shrug. "My father doesn't speak of him, except to compare me to him. And I never win in the comparison. Apparently Leonard was perfect, you see."

"So you're the replacement?" Graham said as he handed over a pole, now ready with a worm on its hook.

James flinched and Simon reached out to slap Graham's arm. "Bloody hell, Graham."

Graham glared at him. "I don't mean it to be cruel."

"And he's right, anyway," James said as he tossed out his

line into the waves. "I'm not the heir, I *am* the replacement. My father will never forgive me for that."

"*That's* why he's so cruel," Simon said softly.

The boys were all silent for a long beat, and then James shrugged. "It's not fair. He's despised me from the moment I was born and wasn't Leonard. Actually, he despises all of us, including Meg and Mother. We're not the family he wanted and he's made it clear from as early as I can recall. He hates *me* so much, he won't even teach me what I need to know, then he screams at me for not knowing it." He shook his head. "I have no idea how to be a duke."

Simon sighed. "*I* do. It's all my father talks about with me, how to be the Duke of Crestwood one day."

Graham nodded. "I, too, get the Duke of Northfield lectures on a regular basis. Mine even come in letter form."

Simon and Graham exchanged a grin, and then Simon's eyes went wide. "Wait, what if we helped you, James?"

James looked at him. "What do you mean, help me?"

"If he won't teach you, why couldn't we?" Graham said, sitting up straighter as he took to Simon's plan. "We could form a little group, a club."

"A Duke Club?" Simon said with a roll of his eyes. "Well, isn't that a little trite?"

"There are quite a few boys in our class who are going to be dukes," James said, setting his pole aside and rising to his feet. "There's Baldwin...Lucas..."

"Hugh...not the future baron Hugh. The Duke of Brighthollow's son Hugh," Graham added. "And a bunch more in classes just below and just above our own."

James rubbed his chin. All these boys, all with their knowledge, all helping each other as they prepared to take what was the highest title of the land without being royalty...just the idea gave him hope.

"We can't call it a Duke Club," James said. "Simon is right that it's silly. But I like the idea of us banding together. Our fathers can be so useless...but together we could be stronger and better than they are."

Simon grinned. "I certainly like that idea. But if not a Duke Club, what do we call it?"

James considered for a moment, then smiled. "The 1797 Club. For its founding year at this creek side."

Graham tilted his head. "I like that."

James let out a laugh, the sting of his father's rejection fading for the first time thanks to the excitement of their plan. He paced the water's edge, his mind racing.

"There will be much to do. We need to figure out who to invite. And what to do. Where to meet..."

Simon laughed. "Well, first you have a fish on your line. So catch that and *then* we'll talk."

James lunged for the jerking pole and began to drag his fish in. But he didn't care about the wriggling beast. He only cared about what plans he and his friends had set in motion.

CHAPTER ONE

1810

One of the most exclusive and expensive parties that had ever opened a London Season was going on around James Rylon, Duke of Abernathe. There was a lively orchestra, and entertainers who floated through the halls, performing magic and other feats of fantasy. There were fine partners to be had in dancing, and for once the wine wasn't watered down.

And he was utterly, completely and unbearably *bored*. Oh, he smiled and chatted, and everyone had always called him the life of any gathering.

But he was *bored*.

He shifted as a group of ladies approached, smiling behind their fans, the mamas pushing to get a good position for their eligible daughters. He forced a pleasant smile onto his face.

"Good evening, ladies," he drawled, searching his mind for names to go with the faces. He would find them, he had no doubt. Surface politeness and perfection were his specialties. What lay beneath was another story, and one he shared with very few others.

They were all talking at once now, tittering every time he said anything even remotely amusing, and he held back a sigh. He only smiled with something close to authenticity when he saw his best friends, Simon, the Duke of Crestwood, and

Graham, the Duke of Northfield, approaching through the crowd. Both had an amused expression at finding him so besieged. Expressions that fell when the ladies caught sight of them and they were drawn into the trap just as he had been.

"There are so many dukes in your generation," cooed one of the young ladies, who batted her eyelashes first at James, then at the other two. "And you're all such good friends."

Simon shrugged. "It is the time of the young duke, I suppose."

"And yet none of you have chosen to marry," one of the mamas said, her lip pushing out in a pout.

"That isn't true," James said, grabbing Graham's arm and all but shoving him into the fray. "Northfield here will marry my sister Margaret. That has been arranged for years."

He could see his words didn't appease the small crowd of ladies, even as they offered a round of half-hearted felicitations nonetheless.

"Perhaps you will excuse us, ladies," Simon said, his voice suddenly a little tight. "We have a bit of business to discuss before we all begin dancing."

The carrot of future dances dangled before them, the ladies smiled and backed away, but James could still feel their stares on him from across the room. He let out a long sigh.

"Are you well?" Simon asked, tilting his head and examining James more closely.

James pressed his lips together. Trust Simon and Graham to see through to the truth. But it wasn't a truth he as yet wanted to discuss. "Of course," he said with a wide smile. "Though I can tell it's going to be a challenging Season if the first night is already so intense."

Simon shrugged as he looked off into the crowd, his expression now as serious as James, himself, felt. "We are of an age, I suppose. The expectations are upon us to wed and produce our heirs. It makes us lambs to a slaughter in rooms like these."

James nodded. Oh yes, he knew of those expectations all too well. They rested heavily on his shoulders, weighing him down even when he was so practiced at pretending to be light and carefree.

"Well, I've no plans to be leg shackled any time soon," he said with a laugh that felt very false. He turned to Graham in the hopes he could change the subject. "I'll leave it to Graham to do the marrying first."

Now his smile was real. When his father died eight years ago, his first act as duke was to arrange a union between Graham and his beloved younger sister, Margaret. He did it to solidify her future, but also so that Graham would be his brother in reality, as much as he was in spirit.

He expected Graham to smile at the talk of his future marriage, but both his friends looked strangely grim. Simon, especially, was now pale and almost looked sick.

"Excuse me, gentlemen, I need a drink," Simon muttered, nodding to them both before he left without waiting for a response.

James stared after him. "What is wrong with him?"

"I don't know," Graham said softly. "He's been out of sorts lately. He refuses to talk to me about it, though."

"Yes, I've noticed the same," James mused.

"See if one of the others can get it out of him," Graham suggested.

James smiled again. The others. Graham was referring to the men in their informal 1797 Club. All men destined to be dukes. They had helped James in so many of his darkest hours. They were the best of men and he was proud to call them friends and allies.

There was Graham and Simon, of course, his very best friends and the ones who had helped him form the group. They had soon asked Baldwin Undercross, now the Duke of Sheffield, to be a part of it. He'd brought along his cousin, Matthew Cornwallis, now Duke of Tyndale. From him, they had added Ewan Hoffstead, who had recently become the Duke of Dunborrow. He was also mute, but he had a keen intellect and was a good friend.

Lucas Vincent, now Duke of Willowby, had joined their set a year later. Now he was no longer in London. Truth be told, no one knew where he was at all, but when he returned James had no doubt he would fall right back into their friendship as if not a day had passed.

Hugh Margoilis, Duke of Brighthollow, and Robert Smithton, Duke of Roseford, had come in after Lucas. Their final member was Christopher Collins, currently the Earl of Idlewood. He was their only member who had not yet inherited his dukedom, though there was no disappointment in that fact, for his father, the Duke of Kingsacre, had been a kind influence on all the men over the years.

It was a large group, but incredibly tight. James knew he could depend on any one of them to help if he needed it. And he couldn't imagine a scenario where anything could tear their longtime friendships apart.

"Why do you ask *me* to see if someone else could get Simon's troubles out of him?" James asked.

Graham arched a brow. "Don't play as if you don't know you're the leader of our little group, James."

James laughed, but he appreciated Graham's informality. When they were alone, Simon and Graham never called him by his title, for they knew Abernathe came with so many negative connotations. Even now, years after the last duke's death, when someone called him by that title, James flinched a little inside and thought of his father's cruelty.

He shook off the thought. "We all have our part, Northfield," he said.

Graham folded his arms and the two of them looked out over the party once more. He shot James a side glance and said, "Are you *really* so opposed to marriage this Season?"

James tensed slightly as Graham was entering dangerous waters. "I'm only seven and twenty. I feel I have plenty of time to do my…duty."

"I suppose that's true," Graham said softly. "Or even to find someone who makes it feel like more than a mere duty. I hear falling in love is coming into great fashion these days."

It took everything in James not to roll his eyes. Love was a foolish notion, after all. He'd never seen it work out for anyone who attempted it. Certainly, his own parents could hardly stand each other. His father had responded to their unhappiness with shouting and the occasional burst of physical violence. His mother had retreated to her bottle.

No, he had no interest in marrying. Not this Season. And very possibly not any Season at all.

"I doubt there is any woman in this room who could tempt me to love, Northfield," he chuckled. "She would have to be quite extraordinary, indeed."

Emma Liston stood against the wall, wishing she could simply fade into the wallpaper and never be seen again. This was a common reaction when she was dragged to a ball, but tonight it felt more powerful than ever. Normally she slid through these things with only her friend Adelaide at her side. They were wallflowers and liked to have good talks.

Tonight, Adelaide was not in attendance and somehow Emma had gotten caught up in a circle of young women who were certainly no friends of hers. While *she* was a mere bluestocking wallflower, Lady Rebecca and Lady Frances were diamonds of the first water. They were pretty and perfect and popular and...*mean*.

And right now their focused attention was across the room as they all stared at the Duke of Abernathe and the Duke of Northfield, who were standing together, engaged in what seemed to be a serious conversation.

"It is *such* a waste!" Lady Rebecca said, twisting one of her perfectly formed black curls around her finger. "One of them already engaged, the other refuses to even *try* to find a bride!"

Emma had been trying very hard not to look at Abernathe

while the other two talked. She had been out in Society for four long years and he was the one person who made her the most nervous. She tried to avoid him and his path as often as possible.

Now, though, she looked at him, dragged to do so by Lady Rebecca's statement that Abernathe refused to do his duty. Emma *knew* why he troubled her. He was ridiculously handsome, for one. Probably the best-heeled man she'd ever laid eyes upon.

He had intense brown eyes and thick dark hair that he wore just a little too long for current fashion. Not that it mattered. Men like Abernathe made fashion, they didn't follow it. He had once worn a certain pattern on his waistcoat two years before and within weeks every other man in Society had copied the piece. Though none had looked quite so fine in it.

But it wasn't just that he was handsome that threw Emma off. It was that he was…golden. He led the pack around him without even noticing he did it. He laughed loud and often, and sometimes inappropriately, and it didn't matter. He took every bet, he raced every race, he even fought every fight. With a normal man, that kind of boldness would have gotten him tossed out of favor on his ear.

And yet Abernathe's legend only grew with each wild act. He could do no wrong.

In short, he was the opposite of everything she was. Where he was popular, she was forgotten. Where he was handsome, she was plain and she knew it. Where he was golden, she was a bluestocking down to her very toes.

And yet, sometimes when Emma looked at him, she saw a sadness in his stare. A brief flash of heartbreak that didn't fit with the confident display of male power he wore about him like a cloak. Those were the moments he made her most nervous, for she knew she'd caught a glimpse of something he didn't want anyone to see. If he knew she did…well, a man like that could destroy a woman like her without even trying.

"I've heard he's said he won't marry this Season, either," Lady Frances said, dragging Emma from her thoughts with her shrill, annoyed tone. She had folded her arms and was all but glaring at Abernathe like he'd committed a personal offense against her.

Emma glanced at him again. "I wonder why?" she whispered, almost more to herself than to them as she thought again of those unintended glimpses of sadness.

Lady Rebecca turned toward her with a laugh. "I would think it wouldn't matter to *you*, Emma, either way."

There was blood in the water now and Lady Frances met Lady Rebecca's eyes with a cruel tilt to her lips that Emma knew too well. She braced herself for whatever was to come next.

"Yes, Emma," Lady Frances cooed, her tone all false niceness. "It isn't as if a woman like *you* would ever catch his eye."

"I've heard Sir Archibald's wife finally died," Lady Rebecca said. "Perhaps you should inquire if he is looking for a wife to take care of those eight children of his."

They used "helpful" tones, but there was no denying the cruelty of them. Emma kept her expression neutral as she said, "I hadn't heard. I'm sorry for his loss and I appreciate your thoughts for me and my future."

Lady Rebecca and Lady Frances each smiled and laughed, then they linked arms and flounced off without another word for Emma. When they were gone, she let out the breath she'd been holding in and muttered, "Rotten cows."

"I've never liked them either."

Emma stiffened at the voice that came from behind her. She slowly turned to see who had overheard her inappropriate outburst. She blushed to find Lady Margaret, the sister of the Duke of Abernathe, standing at her back, a smile brightening her pretty face.

"Lady Margaret," Emma gasped, her breath suddenly gone from her lungs.

Like her brother, Margaret was very well liked. If she hadn't already been engaged to the Duke of Northfield, there was no doubt she would have had dozens of offers of marriage to choose from.

And yet, unlike the women who had just left Emma's side, Margaret had always seemed kind when they interacted. Just as she smiled kindly now.

"I-I shouldn't have said that," Emma said. "Please don't tell them."

Margaret slipped up beside her and laughed. "I try to avoid the two of them, myself. I promise you I would never tell them a word of what *we* think of them."

Emma breathed a sigh of relief. "Thank you." She shifted with discomfort. "Er, how are you enjoying the party?"

"Lady Rockford outdoes herself every year trying to make her debut ball memorable. But she has clowns this year and their makeup is disturbing." Margaret grabbed Emma's arm and pointed toward one of the performers. "See?"

Emma looked and found the clown Margaret referred to. The red of his makeup resembled blood just a little too much. "Oh my, that *is* alarming," she said with a shiver.

Margaret laughed and Emma found herself doing the same. "I swear, next year she'll bring prisoners from Newgate, complete with chains, just to make us all talk."

"Oh dear, I think I'll skip that party," Emma said.

Margaret nodded. "I'll stay home with you." She smiled broadly. "Now tell me…"

"Emma," Emma supplied quickly.

Margaret's brow wrinkled. "I know who you are, my dear. I came over to talk to you, didn't I?"

"Oh," Emma said, blushing. "I assumed you might not remember as we haven't spoken all that much through the years."

Margaret shrugged. "These things are always such a crush. It isn't for lack of wanting to. I've always enjoyed our talks when we have spoken."

Emma tilted her head, uncertain now if she was being teased. "Have you?"

"I have. But tell me, what were you and the other two

discussing that made you so cross with them?"

Emma bit her lip, uncertain how to proceed. She'd never been much of a liar, but it felt unseemly to tell Margaret that the ladies had been discussing her own brother.

"Well…" she began.

Margaret's eyebrow arched. "Abernathe," she suggested.

Emma felt blood rush to her cheeks. "Yes," she whispered. "How did you know?"

"Everyone is *always* talking about James," Margaret sighed, and Emma wasn't certain if she was upset or resigned or angry at that fact.

"But almost always in a good way, my lady," Emma said swiftly.

"Oh please, call me Meg," Margaret said. "All my friends do."

"Meg. Of course."

"Let me guess, they were discussing my brother's reluctance to marry?" Meg continued.

Emma nodded. "Lady Frances said she heard he will not marry this Season. They were quite disappointed in that potential outcome. He's, as you know, considered quite a catch for women like them."

"Women like them," Meg mused. "Nasty title hunters? I hope he won't marry someone like that. If he marries at all."

"Is that *truly* a possibility?" Emma asked with a shake of her head. "That he would not marry?"

Meg shrugged. "When he thinks I am not listening, he sometimes says things that make me think he is pondering a life lived alone, yes."

Emma just barely kept her mouth from dropping open in surprise. It was a ridiculous notion that a man like Abernathe would refuse to do his duty. More than that, he could have virtually any woman he desired. Any one of them would fall at his feet if he asked for their hand. And any woman he so much as looked at would have the entire focus of Society on her.

"Your mother must be upset at that notion," Emma said,

shivering as she thought of her own mother. Violet Liston was a ball of manic energy, and when she began to roll down a hill toward Emma, there was no escaping her schemes.

Currently her focus was on seeing Emma married. This Season. As soon as was humanly possible.

Meg's face fell. "My mother is…*different* from others. I doubt she would care what James did or didn't do."

Emma tried not to show any reaction on her face. She sometimes heard little whispers about the Dowager Duchess of Abernathe, but never anything entirely untoward.

She shifted and fought to find some way to change the subject from the obviously uncomfortable one. "*You* will marry, though, and soon from what everyone says."

Meg smiled, but there was a tightness to her lips. "Yes, I suppose it shall be soon. Northfield and I cannot be engaged forever. My brother is insistent that we make a date for later this year or early next at the latest."

Emma stared. She'd hoped she would find a more positive subject with Meg's engagement. After all, everyone knew that the Duke of Northfield was one of the Duke of Abernathe's closest friends. He and Meg had practically grown up together and their marriage had been arranged for years.

And yet Meg's smile was false and her eyes dull as the subject was broached. Emma barely resisted the urge to shake her head in disbelief. Here *she* was, her mother pushing her to find a match, her prospects weak at best, nonexistent at worst, and Meg had a duke in her pocket, a man who would let her want for nothing…and she was unsatisfied.

She would never understand the popular.

She sought yet another subject, but before she could find one, someone bumped into Meg and Emma from behind. Both of them turned and Emma was shocked to find the Dowager Duchess of Abernathe, herself, standing behind them. She had a drink in her hand and it sloshed in her glass as she staggered.

"Well, well, well," the duchess said. "If it isn't my dutiful daughter."

Emma caught her breath as she looked toward Meg and saw the color draining from her cheeks. *This* was what Meg had meant by her mother being different, apparently. And suddenly Emma understood a great many things she hadn't fully grasped before.

CHAPTER TWO

"Meg, I've been looking for you," the Duchess of Abernathe said, rather too loudly. She slugged down another gulp of her drink before she hiccupped.

Meg's face had now lost all color, and she stepped forward. "Mother, I thought we talked about how much you would have to drink tonight," she whispered with a quick look toward Emma.

Emma's eyes went wide at this entirely unexpected development. Indeed, the duchess did look deep in her cups. Her eyes were bleary and her body swung.

"You aren't my mother, Margaret Elizabeth Elinor Rylon," the duchess slurred. "You can't tell me what to do while you sit on that high horse of yours."

A few in the crowd close to them were beginning to stare and Meg clutched at her mother's arm. "Please lower your voice."

"Embarrassed, are you?" the duchess hiccupped again.

Emma stared. No lady she knew would make such a scene at a ball, of all things. She had no idea what to do. She could turn away so that Meg wouldn't have to be even more embarrassed, but then she'd leave the other woman to deal with the situation herself. She knew how horrible it could be to have others watch you, talk about you.

She shivered at the thought, and in that moment she made a

"Your Grace," she said with a bright smile. "You may not know me, but I'm Emma Liston, a friend of your daughter's. We were about to go to the retiring room to rest a moment. Perhaps you would like to join us."

Meg jerked her face toward Emma and she nodded slightly as if to encourage her. "Yes, Mother. The retiring room is just the place."

The duchess looked entirely confused as Meg removed the glass from her mother's hand, set it aside and then she and Emma each took one of her arms. They began to lead her through the crowd, holding her up as she stumbled in her growing stupor.

"Don't fall," Emma heard Meg whispering through clenched teeth. "Oh, please, don't fall and let them see."

Emma was flooded with a sense of empathy for the other woman. She understood what it was like to have a parent who humiliated her. She understood the fear that engrained, the anxiety. Only it was her father who did it to her, rather than her mother.

She caught a glimpse of a few in the crowd staring and cleared her throat. "Oh yes, Your Grace, it *is* dreadfully hot, isn't it? The retiring room will be just the place to recover your senses."

Meg shot her yet another grateful look as those in the crowd went back to what they were doing. But as they exited the room, Meg looked over her shoulder. Emma didn't know what she was doing, so focused was she on keeping the duchess upright, but within moments of them exiting the ballroom and going into the hall toward the little chamber where the ladies went to rest, there were heavy footsteps behind them.

Emma glanced over her shoulder and her heart nearly stopped as she saw the Duke of Abernathe at her very heel. His usually bright and confident expression had been replaced with one of concern.

"Meg," he said softly.

Emma's heart skipped without her wishing it to have that

reaction. He had such a deep, resonating voice, one that hit her in the stomach and then trailed little flutters even lower.

An entirely inappropriate reaction when she was dragging his drunken mother away from the eyes of Society. She pushed the reaction away and refocused.

"Yes," Meg said, answering a question he hadn't asked.

He frowned as he opened the retiring room door and allowed Meg, Emma and the dowager to enter. It was empty, thank goodness, and Emma and Meg helped the duchess to a settee where she collapsed, grinning up at them.

"I like your friend, Meg," she slurred. "Gemma, you may not be a great beauty, but you have spark."

Meg gasped. "Mother! Enough." She turned to face Emma. "I'm so sorry."

Emma reached out to take Meg's hand, trying desperately to ignore Abernathe as he stood at the door to the room, arms folded, gaze focused on the little show before him. "You have nothing to be sorry about. I-I should leave you. But I hope your mother feels better."

Meg blinked at tears and nodded. "Yes, thank you again for your help, your *kindness*, Emma."

Emma squeezed her hand and then turned toward the door. Abernathe was staring at her now, his dark gaze focused on her face as she took a few hesitant steps toward him.

"Y-Your Grace," she whispered, her voice cracking.

He nodded at her. "Thank you, Miss..."

He trailed off and she whispered, "Liston, Emma Liston."

"Miss Liston," he said.

Then his focus was gone, back to the family drama unfolding on the fainting couch across the room. Emma left them, shutting the door behind her and leaned against it, trying to catch her breath.

What had just happened was certainly not what she expected as she entered the ball tonight. Somehow she had involved herself with one of the most powerful families in Society. Somehow she'd come to know a secret about them.

Now she could only hope it wouldn't come back to haunt her.

James scowled as he watched his carriage pull away from the drive. Deep, abiding anger pulsed within him as he turned back toward Meg, who was standing in the foyer, face pale and pinched.

How he hated to see her that way. It brought back memories from their childhood. Memories of taking care of their mother on dozens of nights when she'd lost herself like this. Memories of Meg's pained face when their father had ignored or chastised her. They'd only ever really had each other to rely on. When she was hurt, James felt as though he'd failed her somehow.

"I should have gone with her," Meg said.

James shook his head. "Mother had Miss Watson with her," he said, referring to their mother's lady's companion. "And she was so apologetic that she allowed Mother to drink too much, I'm certain she will take good care of her."

"Your carriage may not survive the trip home," Meg mused, though her tone was anything but humorous.

"It can be cleaned if she casts up her accounts," he said with another frown. "Are *you* all right?"

"She hasn't made a scene in public like that in years," Meg whispered. "Thank God Miss Liston was there. She helped me enormously."

James nodded as he thought of Emma Liston. He'd seen her before at these things, though he had to admit she'd never caught his eye. He generally turned his attention toward showy women, ones who played along with the games of Society.

Miss Liston was a wallflower. He knew that about her. Her brown hair and her slender frame weren't the kind of physical attributes he normally swung toward when he felt like flirting. But there had been one thing about her that had stood out. She had blue-green eyes. He'd never seen a color quite like them before. Lovely eyes.

"Is she the kind who would talk?" he asked, drawing his mind back to the matter at hand. "That little scene Mother created could easily gain a woman like that some interest if she chose to share it."

Meg wrinkled her brow. "I don't think so. I admit, I don't know her very well, but there was nothing but kindness in the way she handled it. She even took the attention off Mother as we were moving through the crowd."

James nodded slowly. "Then we owe her our thanks. But please don't let Mother ruin your night, Meg. Go dance with Graham."

Meg stiffened ever so slightly. "Northfield doesn't care to dance, you know that."

James frowned. "Then dance with Simon. He's always up for a turn."

Meg turned her face away a moment. "Very well, I shall see if Simon will dance. But only if you make me a promise."

"What is that?" he asked, smiling at her. "You know it is almost impossible for me to refuse you."

"*Almost,*" she repeated with a small smile of her own. "Will *you* dance with Emma?"

"Meg—" he began.

She lifted her eyebrow in accusation. "After what she just did to help us, you would refuse her? Honestly, James, it's a dance. You know if you do it, her card will likely fill for the night. We owe her that, don't we?"

He nodded slowly. "Very well, I shall dance with Miss Emma Liston. At the very least, it will give me a chance to determine if she will say anything about Mother's…state tonight."

Meg frowned as they two of them fell into step back toward the ballroom. "If you need an ulterior motive, then by all means, James."

He caught her arm before she moved into the crowd to find

Simon. "Save one for me, too, will you?"

The tightness in his sister's face faded and she leaned up to kiss his cheek lightly. "Always."

She turned away and moved into the crowd, leaving James standing at the edge of the room. He looked into the milling group of people, all dressed in their finery. Right now, after that scene with his mother, he wanted nothing more than to go home to his bed.

But he had a part to play and a promise to keep to his sister. So he stepped out into the crowd to find Emma Liston. He did so quickly enough. She was standing in the corner, at the wall, her face taut with emotion. He set his shoulders back as he made his way across the room toward her.

The closer he got, the more he paid attention to her. It wasn't just her eyes that were pretty. She had a fine mouth, as well, with full lips. Lips that parted when she turned her head to find him coming toward her.

She straightened up as he reached her. "Y-Your Grace," she stammered.

"Miss Liston," he said with a nod of his head. "I wondered if you'd like to have a dance with me, if your card is not already full."

She stiffened at that statement and a guard lifted between them. Her tone became cool as she said, "This dance is open, yes."

He held out an arm and she hesitated slightly before she slid her slender hand into the crook of his elbow. He was surprised by the shock of awareness that crackled through him at the action. He felt every single one of her fingers against his body, smelled a faint scent of lilac from her hair, heard the swish of her skirt as it brushed his leg.

He blinked. He *was* on edge if he was noticing such things. He pushed them away and guided her to the dancefloor for the first waltz of the evening. Immediately, he felt dozens of pairs of eyes swing toward them and a ripple went through the crowd.

Miss Liston seemed to notice it, too, for she stumbled in the first step and he tightened his grip of her to keep her from falling.

She looked up apologetically. "I don't often waltz," she explained.

He ignored the statement as they turned through the crowd. "You were a great help with the...situation with my mother tonight," he said softly.

Her lips parted again in surprise and he had a flash of a moment where he wondered what they would taste like. He shook his head again to clear his mind. Damn, but he was rattled by his mother's actions.

"Everyone gets overheated from time to time at a ball," Miss Liston said carefully. "I was happy to be of assistance. I hope she is feeling better."

"She is going home," he said. "And we both know she wasn't merely overheated."

She swallowed hard and looked up to meet his gaze. Once again he was struck by how stunning her eyes were. He didn't think he'd ever seen such a combination of blue and green before.

"If anyone asked me," she said slowly, "that would be what I would tell them. It is all I recall, at any rate."

He wrinkled his brow at her reassurance, kindly made and somehow unexpected. "If you said something else, it might bring you a little renown."

Her eyes narrowed. "Please don't presume you know me well enough to believe I would trade renown for someone else's reputation, Your Grace. I didn't help your sister or your mother in order to gain something from the act. There *is* decency without price in this world. If you do not know that, I am sorry for you."

James arched a brow at her heated response. When she was emotional, she was far more animated and a blush crept into her cheeks and down her neck, disappearing into the bust of her gown.

"I apologize, Miss Liston," he said, inclining his head. "I did not mean to imply that you would be mercenary. Truly."

Her expression softened a touch. "I'm sure there are some who might be. I'm simply not one of them."

"Then we are lucky *you* were the friend my sister was with," he said. "And once again, I thank you."

"Your sister is lovely," Miss Liston said, looking over his shoulder into the crowd of other dancers.

When he turned her, he saw that Meg was dancing with Simon. She was smiling and laughing, and his heart got lighter seeing it.

"She is, indeed," he said. "She likes you."

The music had begun to slow and Miss Liston looked up at him with wide eyes. "Does she? I cannot imagine why. We do not have anything in common."

He laughed at her candor, even if he didn't believe her words. "You are both clever. And clearly you are both kind. That is the foundation of many a friendship, Miss Liston."

The music stopped and he bowed to her, then offered her a hand to escort her from the floor. When they reached the edge, he swept the cloak of his personality around him and said, "It was a great pleasure to dance with you, Miss Liston. I hope you will allow me the pleasure again."

To his surprise, she didn't titter as other women might have. Instead, she folded her arms across her chest like a shield and pressed those surprisingly full lips together until they were a tight line.

"Your Grace, we both know this was a pity dance, thrown at me as some kind of reward for my help. And clearly it was also a way to determine if I would use whatever I saw tonight against you. Please don't pretend it was something more. I understand the way the world works."

He drew back. "You *are* direct."

Panic flooded her face and she shifted with discomfort. "Well, a woman of my position must be practical and not allow herself to get swept away by foolish notions."

"Like that I could have actually enjoyed dancing with you?" he asked with a slight smile. "It is so hard for you to believe."

She shrugged. "I'm not exactly in your sphere, Your Grace."

"Miss Liston, whether you believe it or not, I *did* truly enjoy my time with you," he said, and was surprised to find he actually meant those words. Normally when he danced with ladies, he went through the motions, trying to be polite while he awaited escape. This dance had been different. Emma Liston was...*interesting*.

She bent her head. "Well, I...I...thank you. Now I should go find my mother. Good night, Your Grace."

He inclined his head. "Good night, Emma."

She stiffened at the use of her given name, but she didn't correct him before she turned away and rushed off through the crowd, leaving James alone to watch her. And watch her he did, until she vanished into the crowd and left him entirely confused by their encounter.

CHAPTER THREE

Emma stared at her plate with unseeing eyes. What did her rapidly cooling food matter when all she could do was relive her dance with the Duke of Abernathe again and again? Like a fool, she kept thinking of his strong arms around her, the warmth of his body as they spun around the floor, the focus of his dark stare as he spoke to her.

Of course, she'd ruined it all by being so damned direct with him.

"Emma!"

She jerked her head up to find her mother leaning across the table, eyes locked on her. Emma sighed. She knew that look. It was the *marry, marry, marry* look that made her mother so crazed sometimes.

"I'm sorry, Mama," Emma said. "I was woolgathering."

Violet Liston smiled. "Daydreaming about the Duke of Abernathe? Oh, Emma, I cannot tell you how thrilled I am that you caught his attention."

Emma pursed her lips before she muttered, "Really? I wasn't aware when you mentioned it ten times last night and at least four this morning."

"No need to be cheeky," Mrs. Liston scolded. "The night was a smashing success. You haven't had so much attention in years."

Emma frowned, for she couldn't deny her mother's charge.

After Abernathe had left her, she *had* been approached by several other gentlemen. Not of Abernathe's stature, of course, but what her mother would call "viable options." It had been a long time since her dance card had more than two names on it. Last night, she had ended up with five.

"It was just a few dances, Mama," she said, pushing her plate away since she had no appetite.

"A few dances is the path to a marriage," her mother insisted, fisting her napkin in her hand on the tabletop. Emma saw how white her knuckles were, and her frown deepened.

"Don't buy my trousseau too soon, Mama," she said gently. "I am still a spinster."

Her mother turned her face as if that word were a curse. In this house, it sometimes felt like it was. "How can you be so cavalier, Emma," she snapped. "You know our circumstances. Your father—"

"Is not here," Emma interrupted. "And has not been here for six months."

"But he always returns," Mrs. Liston said, rising to her feet and pacing the dining room restlessly. "And when he does, he regularly brings a scandal with him. We've done well covering them up, keeping their glare off you, but there will come a point when I cannot protect you anymore. But if you are already safely married before his next...outburst, then it won't matter. You *must* see how important that is, Emma."

Emma closed her eyes and let out a long breath before she looked at her mother again. "I see how important you *feel* it is," she whispered. "But Mama, what would happen if I simply remained an old maid?"

Mrs. Liston's mouth twisted in horror and she stepped toward Emma. Her tone grew loud and wild as she cried, "Are you so naïve? The money we have cannot stretch forever."

"Not in the lifestyle we maintain now, no," Emma conceded. "But if we stopped focusing on my Seasons and took a smaller home in the countryside—"

Her mother folded her arms. "You do not care about me,"

she interrupted, her lip trembling and her eyes welling with tears. "You don't *want* to take care of me. You don't *care* if I am humiliated."

With that her mother rushed from the room, wailing all the way up the stairs. The sound faded away until there was a great slamming of Mrs. Liston's chamber door. Emma placed her elbows on the table and rested her head in her hands.

She was accustomed to these outbursts from her mother. Mrs. Liston had married the third son of an important family and they had a complicated relationship. When Harold Liston was around, Emma's mother cooed and purred over him. He could do no wrong.

But when he left, Mrs. Liston suddenly recalled all his many faults. It had never been a secret that she had hoped to elevate herself with the match. But Emma's father had long ago been cut off from his influential relatives. She and her mother were only on the fringes of good Society.

Emma had always accepted that fact. Her mother could not, and more and more over the years, she had pinned her hopes on Emma's own future match. The longer Emma stayed unwed, the more frustrated her mother became.

It wasn't that Emma never wanted to marry from the beginning. She'd had dreams of finding someone nice, someone who cared for her and who she could care for. But the truth of Society had crushed that out of her within her first Season.

Most men cared about what they could obtain from a match. Most women knew how to play the game better than she did. And so her spinsterhood had begun.

If it were just her, she could live with it. She would do exactly as she'd just suggested to her mother and move to a smaller home, stop investing in gowns and other frivolity and live out her life with books and a cat and a good friend or two to call on from time to time.

But the idea of a life lived with her mother haranguing her over her failure to make a good match was not a pleasant idea.

She stood up and paced to the fire. As she did so, her maid,

Sally, entered the room. Emma faced her with a sigh. "Let me guess, my mother sent you to me with a message that I've broken her heart."

Sally nodded with a tight smile. "Yes, miss."

Emma rolled her eyes. "Great God, it's so predictable."

"She only wants to see you settled, miss. Happy."

Emma wasn't certain that was exactly true, but she didn't argue. "I suppose."

"Is it true you danced with the Duke of Abernathe?" Sally asked.

Emma shook her head. Abernathe was so powerful, so charismatic, even the servants got a flutter to their voices when he was discussed. "I did. *And* a few others."

She paused as she considered those words. Her mother had said something about the attention Emma had gotten thanks to Abernathe. And while Emma had dismissed it aloud, she couldn't pretend that Mrs. Liston wasn't right. What Abernathe wanted, paid attention to, became fashion. Clothes, drinks…women.

Was it possible she *could* leverage his temporary regard into a match of some kind?

Before she could ponder the idea much further, their butler, Kendall, entered the breakfast room. "Miss Liston, a missive for you."

Emma crossed the room to take it. She turned it over and caught her breath. It was the seal of the House of Abernathe. Her hands shook a little as she broke it and unfolded the pages.

It was an invitation to a garden party in two days' time and scrawled across the more formal page was a note from Meg. *Please do come!*

Emma drew in a long breath as the butler left the room. "How long will it take Kendall to report this to my mother?"

Sally laughed. "Three minutes," she guessed. "And that's only because he's slow climbing the stairs."

Emma stared at the looping, friendly message from Meg. Meg, who claimed to like her. And she shook her head.

"Well, then I suppose I'm going to a garden party," she said.

"Excellent," Sally said. "I'll be sure you have a few gowns to pick from. And your mother will be pleased."

Her maid slipped from the room and left Emma alone. She rubbed her eyes and sighed. "Oh yes, Mama will be over the moon."

But as for herself, she was left with a restless feeling. One that had nothing to do with gardens or parties or Meg. One that had everything to do with Abernathe.

As Meg entered his office, James looked up from his pile of paperwork and smiled at her. When he saw her face, pale and pinched, his expression fell and he rose to his feet.

"What is it?" he asked.

Meg reached behind her, sliding his door shut before she leaned on it with a sigh. "My garden party starts in half an hour," she said.

He nodded. "Yes?"

"And Mother is drunk. Again."

He shut his eyes and shook his head. Anger rose up in his chest, but he tamped it down and instead looked at his sister. "I'm sorry, Meg."

She let her head rest against the door a moment and he could see she was fighting frustrated tears. "She does well for months at a time and then she spirals into this. I know her life has not been happy, I know Father was... *Father*. He made it plain to all of us how much he despised us and wished we were those he truly loved. I want to have understanding for how broken that made her, but I am so *incredibly* frustrated by her behavior."

James moved around the desk and came to fold his arms around her. He felt her go limp for a moment before she regained her strength. She looked up at him with a sad smile.

"What can I do?" he asked as she pulled from his embrace.

She met his stare. "Will you...will you come out and say hello?"

"Margaret," he said, turning his back to go sit at his desk again.

"Don't Margaret me!" she said, but laughter had returned to her tone. "Please, it will put the ladies all in a twitter and take some of the focus off Mother's absence."

He pressed his lips together and then glared at her. "You use my absolute adoration of my baby sister against me."

She grinned. "Every single time, yes."

He threw up his hands in surrender. "Very well. I shall poke my head out. But I warn you, I will make an excuse to go. I have things on my agenda today that cannot be ignored."

She clapped her hands together and there was no denying the relief on Meg's face. "Oh, thank you, Jamie."

He smiled at the shortening of his name, a throwback to their childhood days. Margaret so rarely called him that anymore and it warmed him. "You're welcome."

"You may change your mind about not staying," she said as she moved toward the door.

He sighed. "And why would I do that? I have no interest in listening to your friend's gossip."

Meg rolled her eyes at him. "We do more than gossip. And the reason you may wish to stay is that someone you like will be there."

He shook his head in confusion. "Someone I like? You?"

"No. Emma Liston," Meg said, laughing as she exited the room and left James alone with her parting words. He leaned back in his chair, staring after her.

Emma Liston. It had been two days since he last saw her at Lord and Lady Rockford's Season opening ball. He'd been trying hard to get her out of his mind ever since. It was a funny thing that she kept popping into his head. She wasn't at all his type and he hardly ever thought much of one woman over another.

"It is likely because she saw Mother at her worst and offered kindness," he muttered, looking back down at the ledger before him. Now the numbers swam and he could hardly recall what he was doing before Meg came in and distracted him.

Certainly it wasn't thoughts of Emma Liston that did that. Certainly not. Nor was she the reason that this chore to go say hello to Meg's guests suddenly seemed less irritating.

No. Not at all.

As the carriage rounded the last bend onto the drive at the Duke of Abernathe's London estate, Emma swallowed hard and tried to maintain some small semblance of calm. It wasn't easy when across from her, Mrs. Liston was talking on and on, just as she had been since they left their home nearly half an hour before.

"You should try to sit next to Lady Margaret," her mother said.

Emma shook her head. "Mama, I'm certain there will be seating arrangements made and more important guests will be seated next to Meg—Lady Margaret."

Her mother's eyes lit up in triumph. "Well, make sure you talk to her for as long as you can, regardless. She could be your champion."

Emma gripped her hand on the carriage seat. "Mama, I don't want to use—"

"Posh!" her mother interrupted, waving one hand wildly. "Of course you should use this connection. It could be your saving grace."

"Please, Mama," Emma whispered, exhaustion washing over her in one long wave. "Just, *please*."

The carriage stopped before they could continue the argument and her mother shot her one more pointed glare before she was helped from the carriage by a footman. Emma smoothed her skirts, tried to calm her suddenly racing heart, and followed Mrs. Liston out of the vehicle.

As she looked up at the fine home, she was surprised as Meg, herself, stepped from the front door and waved at them from the top step.

Mrs. Liston grabbed Emma's arm and all but dragged her up to the top, chattering all the time.

"Lady Margaret!" she called out. "How lovely of you to invite us. You know how Emma cherishes your friendship, we are so pleased."

Emma's cheeks flared with heat at her mother's over-solicitous words. She cast Meg a quick look but found the other woman didn't look irritated by the silliness of her guest.

"The pleasure is all mine, I assure you," Meg said, reaching out to catch Emma's hand for a brief squeeze. "Hello, Emma."

"My lady," Emma said softly, reverting back to correct formality for this public setting as she met Meg's stare.

For a flash she saw understanding in her eyes. A bond made by mothers who humiliated their daughters, though in very different ways. And for the first time that day, she drew a full breath and calmed a little.

"You two are our last arrivals," Meg said, sliding an arm through Emma's. "So I shall escort you back to the veranda myself."

Emma gasped in horror at that statement. Her mother had forced her to change three times, then ultimately had her put on the first dress she'd started with, a yellow gown with blue flowers stitched through the bodice. Of course, that was why they had run late.

"I'm so sorry to delay the party," Emma gasped.

Meg shook her head. "Gracious, it's fine. Truly, the previous guest only arrived five minutes ago, so you are not so very tardy. And I'm pleased that our group is now complete."

As she spoke, she took them through a beautiful parlor and out a set of open French doors onto a veranda. Emma couldn't help it. She came to a sudden stop as she looked across the beautiful space.

It was wide and broad with lattices strewn with flowering vines. From this vantage point one could see the sprawling garden behind the estate manor, complete with a rose maze and a huge gazebo off in the distance. There was a fountain in the middle of it all, where a stone lady dressed in flowing Grecian robes poured a never-ending pitcher of water while white angels lifted their hands to catch the liquid.

"Isn't it lovely?" Meg said with a wide smile. "It is one of my favorite places in all the world."

Emma nodded, all but speechless. Then she found herself moving forward as Meg pulled her into the center of the veranda. A dozen tables had been set there, with white table clothes and beautiful floral arrangements in the center of each. They were full now with finely dressed ladies chatting and smiling. Emma saw a few look toward her with surprise. Of course they would be surprised—she was never invited to such events.

"Mrs. Liston, I have put you here," Meg said, stopping at a table with one empty seat at it. "I'm certain you already know the ladies."

Emma watched as her mother's eyes all but bugged. The table was filled with some of the most important older women of Society. From the Countess of Hastingcross, who almost singlehandedly dictated the fashions of the day, to the Viscountess Breckinridge, whose annual masquerade ball was the most sought after invitation of any in Society.

"Welcome, Mrs. Liston," Lady Hastingcross said, patting the empty chair beside her. "Your hat is divine."

Mrs. Liston said nothing else to Emma and Meg, but floated into her chair and immediately launched into a discussion with the others. Emma's heart swelled at the opportunity Meg had somehow created for her mother.

But she could see there was no place for her at the table and Meg was already drawing her to another seat closer to the edge of the veranda.

"And you shall sit beside me," Meg said, releasing Emma as she smiled at the ladies who would join them. "Do you know everyone?"

She proceeded to introduce the circle of six others. Emma knew a few but not all, for just as at her mother's table, they were women who ranked far above her in Society. And like with her mother, each woman was friendly and accepting, and Meg helped along the conversations with lively tales. By the way she included Emma in each discussion, it was obvious she had claimed her as a friend and that seemed to be enough for the others in attendance to welcome her into their circle.

The time flew by as tea and treats were served and good conversation was had. Emma was just beginning to feel comfortable when one of the ladies said, "Margaret, darling, where is your mother?"

"Oh yes," said another. "I know she left the Rockford ball early—is she well?"

Emma swallowed and sent Meg a quick look. Her friend had paled a shade and her smile now seemed forced rather than natural. "I'm afraid Mother took a bit ill that night and she is not fully recovered."

"Oh, what a shame," another woman sighed. "You know, I could recommend my physician. He works wonders, you know."

Meg's cheek twitched a fraction and Emma knew the truth in an instant. She so wanted to reach out and squeeze Meg's hand, comfort her, but she resisted.

"Thank you, I shall get his name from you later," Meg said.

If there were to be more questions about the absent duchess, they were cut off as the veranda door opened. Emma turned toward it and caught her breath as the Duke of Abernathe stepped from the house and onto the balcony.

His appearance sent a ripple through the crowd and all chatter increased briefly and then stopped as they stared at him. He grinned, like he was soaking up all the female attention, and came forward.

"Good afternoon, ladies," he all but purred.

Greetings were called out by the large group, but Emma stayed mute. She even found herself sliding down in her chair a bit, praying he wouldn't look at her. Though what she thought would happen if he did was entirely unclear. Would she suddenly glow? Would there be a beacon that lit up above her head and spelled out that she was a fool?

The man probably didn't even recall meeting her or dancing with her at this point. It wasn't as if she was important in any way.

He swung his gaze around the veranda just as those thoughts passed through her mind, and suddenly his dark gaze pierced her. He held on her a long moment, the corner of his lip quirking up as he did so. And then his gaze moved on.

And yet in that moment her heart skipped a beat. Her stupid, foolish, idiot heart leapt at just one look from him. Why in the world did she allow that? He was just a man. A handsome man, yes, but so entirely out of her league that she was silly to even look at him, let alone let her body react with attraction.

"I wanted to say hello," he said. "For how could I resist such a gathering of beauty?"

The group laughed and there were blushes and giggles into fans. Emma watched him smile at the group at large and ducked her head. Of course none of his regard was truly focused on her. It was a trick of the mind, nothing more, seeing something where there was nothing. The man had only danced with her out of some sense of obligation.

She settled back as he spoke a few more words, then exited the veranda back into the house. As soon as he was gone, the party all but exploded as the women talked about him. Even their own table didn't seem to be deterred by the presence of the duke's sister as they buzzed about how handsome Abernathe was and mused on the possibilities of his matching that Season.

Emma ignored it all, staring out across the veranda toward the brief glimpses of green grass and flowers out in the garden. In this moment, she knew she had to stay calm. Stay reasonable. She had to keep herself from being swept up in the general obsession with the Duke of Abernathe. For some lucky lady, he would one day be her husband.

But not Emma.

CHAPTER FOUR

As the party slowly broke apart, Emma shifted. Ever since Abernathe had come out to say his hellos to the group, she had felt out of sorts. Now she just wanted to go home and forget she'd seen him.

But her mother had fallen into a deep conversation with Lady Breckinridge and there seemed no chance they would leave until Mrs. Liston had wrung every opportunity from the new friendship.

Emma turned to watch Meg walk back onto the veranda after she had escorted some of her guests out. Meg smiled as she headed toward Emma.

"Did you have a good time?" her hostess asked.

"Yes," Emma lied. "Thank you so much for inviting us."

Meg slid an arm through hers and guided her away from the crowd. Once they were out of earshot of the few left, she said, "I wondered if you might like to stay a little longer once the others go."

Emma blinked. "Stay here?"

Meg nodded. "Yes. I wanted so much to talk to you more and with everyone here and my hostess duties, it was nearly impossible."

Emma opened her mouth, but didn't get a chance to respond as her mother approached the two. "What are you ladies chatting about so conspiratorially?"

"I am trying to convince your daughter to stay a bit longer, once the others go," Meg said. "I want to take a long turn in the garden and I'd love her company."

Emma saw Mrs. Liston's eyes light up at the idea of getting to stay in the Abernathe home a bit longer. "A fine idea," she said, nudging Emma none too gently.

"I would, of course, ensure she got home safely," Meg added.

Mrs. Liston hesitated a moment as she realized Meg's invitation didn't actually extend to her. But then she recovered and nodded. "Well, of course Emma will stay."

She shot Emma a pointed look, one filled with years of spoken and unspoken haranguing, and Emma held back a sigh. "Of course I will stay, my lady. Thank you."

Meg clapped her hands. "Excellent. Let me see the last of the others out and I'll return shortly."

Emma nodded and her mother leaned forward to buss her cheek. "Take advantage," she whispered sharply in Emma's ear.

"Goodbye, Mama," Emma returned through clenched teeth.

Meg took Mrs. Liston and the others out, and Emma walked to the stone wall of the veranda, resting her hands on the edge to look out over the garden once more. She lost herself for a moment in the cool greenness of the flowers, but reality returned soon enough.

What could Meg wish to speak to her about? Something to do with Lady Abernathe's untoward behavior two nights before? Or was she going to warn Emma off the duke, himself? Had her dance with him been marked by his sister?

"Isn't it lovely?" Meg called as she returned to the veranda. "I cannot wait for you to see it more closely."

Emma turned and stared at the other woman as she approached. She'd spent a lifetime observing those of Meg's stature and popularity. A lifetime trying to avoid their attention because it was rarely positive. Diamonds and wallflowers were simply not friends, not in her experience.

"May I ask you something?" Emma asked, finding her

courage.

Meg nodded. "Of course."

Emma cleared her throat. Normally she wasn't bold, but in this case she found a strong desire to be. To simply lay the cards on the table and see what Meg's real motives were.

"I'm a wallflower. And a bluestocking," she said. "And you're *not*. Wh-why would you want to spent time with me?"

Meg drew back. "Well, because I like you, silly. I think despite those labels we might actually have a great deal in common."

"Like what?" Emma asked blankly, not seeing Meg's reference at all. "I'm sorry to sound rude, I don't mean to be. It's just that I'm confused."

Meg's smile fell a fraction. "Do you not think my intellect is equal to yours?"

Emma shook her head, for it was perfectly clear from some of their conversations today that Meg was anything but an empty-headed ninny. "No. No, of course not."

Meg stepped forward and wrapped an arm around Emma's shoulder. The half-embrace was warm and Meg's smile was sincere as she said, "Emma Liston, you were kind to me in a dark moment. You could have used that moment against me and it doesn't seem that you will. I appreciate that. And I *want* to be friends, for there are few enough of those in this world. Is that enough of a reason for me to ask you to stay?"

Emma pondered for a moment. It seemed Meg was in no way mocking her. And she did like the pretty, bright woman. "Yes," she said softly.

"Excellent," Meg said as she released her. "Now, I'm going to run and fetch a shawl, then we can take a turn in the garden together. Will you stay here?"

Emma nodded. "Yes. I'm enjoying the view a great deal."

"Just wait, it gets even better," Meg said with a laugh as she raced back toward the house.

Emma sighed as she returned her attention to the green expanse before her. She was just beginning to get comfortable when she heard the veranda door shut behind her. When she turned, it wasn't Meg who was reentering the terrace.

It was Abernathe.

James came to a short stop as he looked across the veranda and found Emma Liston at the wall a few feet away. She was staring at him, those entrancing eyes wide. She darted out her tongue to wet her lips before she whispered, "Your Grace" in a husky tone that hit him straight in the gut.

He shook his head slightly. Damn Meg. She'd sent him out to the garden without telling him that Emma was still here.

"Miss Liston," he managed as he strode toward her. "I didn't realize you had stayed."

There was a beat where she seemed to be trying to find words and then she said, "Your sister asked me to remain. She wanted to take a turn around the garden together."

She smiled slightly and James wrinkled his brow. It was the first time he'd seen her smile and though it was not broad, it was a pretty smile. It changed the shape of her face and drew his eyes to her full lips.

"And then she abandoned you," James said. "Bad form, Meg."

Emma took a long step toward him, hand outstretched. "Oh no!" she gasped. "Not at all."

Her true upset at the idea that she would get Meg in trouble warmed him, and he smiled as he ducked his head a little closer. "I was only teasing."

"Oh," she said, her hand dropping back to her side. He found he was a little disappointed in that. He wished she'd touched him. He forced that desire away as she said, "Of course."

"Certainly your brothers must do the same," he said. "It is our prerogative, you know."

She shook her head slowly. "I have no brothers, Your Grace."

"Ah, I see," he said with a grin. "Sisters, then. Poor girl."

She laughed and the small smile became a larger one. James could hardly breathe at the sight of it. Good Lord, that wide expression transformed her into something entirely lovely.

"It is just me, I'm afraid."

He moved another step closer. "Would you like to walk with me?"

The moment he asked the question, he drew back a fraction. Why had he done that?

Emma hesitated and her gaze slid to the doors to the house. James wondered at that beat of reluctance. Most women would have none. He knew a match with him was considered valuable. Especially for a woman in Emma's position.

"You—you needn't trouble yourself," she said at last.

He tilted his head. "It is no trouble, Miss Liston. It would be a pleasure." He held out his arm. "Please."

"And what about your sister? She'll be back any moment and she expects me to be here."

He smiled. "Meg won't fly into a rage, I assure you. And she'll be able to see us from the terrace. I'm certain she'll simply catch up to us and the two of you can carry on with your walk."

She hesitated again, and he was fascinated by the fact that her reluctance made him want her acceptance all the more. Finally she nodded, and it was like he'd won a prize as she took his arm and allowed him to guide her to the stairs that led down to the garden.

She was quiet as they moved toward the pathway through the garden and he said, "It is rare for a family to be so small. No brothers or sisters."

He thought he saw a brief shadow cross her face, and then she said, "Well, my parents were not blessed with more than one child. Your family is little better, though, isn't it? With all your talk of brothers and sisters, it is only you and Meg."

He nodded. "Yes, I suppose that is true. I sometimes

forget."

She laughed as she glanced up at him. "You forget you have no other siblings? That is a fairly large thing to forget, my lord."

He smiled at her teasing. Once again, he was struck by how unlikely it was that another lady of his acquaintance would do the same. They were so often grasping to make an impression, to make a match.

Emma was different. And he found that inspired candor in him that he might not have had with another person.

"I suppose I forget because I have such a tight circle of friends," he explained. "The 1797 Club."

She blinked. "The 1797 Club? I'm not aware of it."

"It is incredibly exclusive," he said, motioning her to a bench that overlooked the fountain in the middle of the garden. She took a place and he sat beside her, suddenly aware of how close their knees were as he spoke.

"So exclusive that it feels like family?" she asked, seemingly oblivious to his thoughts.

"They are my brothers. We formed the little group when we were boys."

"In 1797," she teased. "At the ripe old age of...what? Twelve?"

"Fourteen," he corrected with a nod. "You see, I needed help as I moved toward inheritance of my dukedom. And we formed a group of all of us who would take that same level of title so we could assist each other."

"And how many are you?" she asked.

"Ten, including myself," he said.

She smiled once more, this time gentle and understanding. "Then you have a very large family after all. And that is a lucky and rare thing."

"Yes."

"Is the Duke of Northfield one of those in your group?" she asked.

"He and the Duke of Crestwood were my closest friends as a boy. Together we came up with the idea of the club and it grew over the years that followed."

"And now Northfield will marry Meg," she said. "And become your brother in truth."

"Yes. I admit that was part of the draw of matching them," he said.

"But everyone says *you* will never marry. Of course, likely I won't either. But for different reasons. Yours is a choice and mine—"

With a gasp, she stopped talking. Her eyes went wide and she slapped a hand over her mouth, her gaze flitting over to him and going wide and wild.

Emma wanted nothing more than to sink down under the bench where they sat and disappear for the rest of her life. She had no idea why she had lost control of her tongue. She and Abernathe had been sitting together, having a perfectly lovely conversation. Comfortable, aside from the fact that she couldn't stop contemplating how utterly handsome he was.

And then she'd gone and burst out something inappropriate about his lack of desire for marriage. About her own lack of ability to marry. She was an absolute idiot.

"I'm sorry, Your Grace," she said when she could find enough breath to speak. "That was entirely out of turn."

He was quiet a moment, then he said, "Emma, we were having an honest conversation. I don't mind having an honest conversation with you. But you cannot truly believe that you will never marry."

She pushed to her feet and walked toward the fountain, her hands clenched at her sides. "This is really none of your concern. I forgot myself for a moment. There is nothing else to say."

He followed her forward. "Emma."

She stiffened. That was the third time he'd called her by her given name. She shouldn't like it so much. She *should* correct him.

She opened her mouth to do so when he pierced her with a hard look and asked, "Why do you think you will never marry?"

She gasped for air, for words, and he reached out. Suddenly he had her hand in his. She wasn't wearing gloves, having taken them off for lunch. Neither was he. His skin was rough on hers, his hand a shade darker as it engulfed her own.

"Not everyone is golden," she whispered, her voice almost not her own. Her words coming when she didn't want them to. "I am an old maid, with little to recommend me thanks to…" She trailed off.

"Thanks to?" he encouraged, his dark eyes still intently focused on her. Like he actually gave a damn about the answer.

And for a moment she pondered giving it to him. Pondered spilling out every painful fact of her past and her own fractured family to him. But she caught herself before she could. Whatever spell she was under with this man, she wasn't about to talk about her father with him and give him a reason to laugh at her.

"I'm a spinster and a wallflower," she said, pulling her hand away from his at last and wishing she couldn't still feel the warmth of it. "There is no other reason than that which precludes many women like me from marrying. My mother insists I must wed, of course, to increase our circumstances. She drives me toward it constantly. But it isn't as easy as just waving my hand and having men fall at my feet."

He shook his head slowly. "It's a funny thing. Here I am trying to avoid a marriage trap and you wish to land in one."

"Yes," she said, then covered her face. "God, I feel like such a fool."

"Why?" he said with a laugh.

She lowered her hands and glared at him. "Really? You ask that question of me?"

His joviality faded at her pointed question. "I'm sorry if I was glib," he said, true chagrin on his face. "You helped my sister, helped me. Is there some way I can help you?"

"Pretend to court me in order to make me attractive to some

other man?" she said, then shook her head with a laugh. "No, my lord. There is *nothing* you can do, though I do thank you for your concern."

His brow wrinkled, and for a moment she thought he might say something. But then Meg's voice came drifting over the garden. "James, I was going to show her the fountain!"

James took a long step back from her, and Emma found herself a little colder now that he was gone. Whatever seriousness had been on his face faded, and he turned to his sister with a bright grin. "Well, I beat you to it."

Meg swatted his arm playfully. "You never allow me any boon."

"I'm sorry, Meg," he said. "I shall leave you to your friend." He turned back to Emma with a nod. "Miss Liston, it was a great pleasure."

There was sincerity to his tone and to his expression as he nodded at her. Emma gulped hard and said, "Thank you for your company, Your Grace. Good day."

"Good day," he repeated, then strode off toward the house. Leaving Emma with Meg.

Leaving Emma with a sense of discomfort and a mind full of questions.

CHAPTER FIVE

James stared at his plate, but he was entirely distracted. Since he'd last encountered Emma Liston a few days before, he had relived their conversation in the garden over and over. Not only had he revealed so much about himself, for he hardly ever discussed his band of tight friends with anyone, let alone a stranger...but he had found himself engaged by her.

She was not like anyone he'd ever met before. Where most ladies in his circle focused on how to best present themselves, Emma had a refreshing honesty that drew him in.

He shook his head, pushing thoughts of her away as he looked at his companions. He was sharing supper with Meg and Graham, but neither was talking. Meg pushed her food around her plate with the tines of her fork and Graham was silent.

James cleared his throat. "We are a thrilling group, aren't we?"

Graham grinned at him and Meg straightened up. "We all have something on our minds, it seems," she said, shooting a quick glance at Graham. He didn't return it.

"I know what you two must be thinking of," James said. "We *do* have a wedding to plan."

To his surprise, Meg stiffened a little at the mention of her upcoming nuptials. He frowned. James wasn't certain what was going on with his sister. She'd become increasingly odd as of late. Most women would have been giddy to plan a huge Society wedding to a rich, powerful duke who had been a friend for years. Meg seemed entirely disinterested.

He could only hope that once she and Graham were married, she would calm down a little. Her troubles would fade when she was settled.

"I was actually thinking more about the country party next week," Meg said. "I realize it's already a full house, but I was considering inviting Emma Liston and her mother to fill out the group."

"Emma?" he repeated, all the thoughts he'd been trying to stifle returning.

She nodded. "We had a wonderful time a few days ago. I do like her, James. And I think we could be of help to her, as well."

James's errant mind took him back, once again to their conversation in the garden a few days before. Emma had so much tension on her face when she spoke of needing to wed, of the complications of that drive.

"James?" Meg asked, intruding into his thoughts.

"Very well," he said with a shake of his head. "I see no reason why not. We have the room."

She smiled and rose, forcing Graham and him to do the same. "Excellent. While you and Graham have your port, I'll write her an invitation. And then I'll likely retire early." She partially turned toward her fiancé. "Good night, Graham."

Graham stepped toward her, but did not take her hand. He merely executed a stiff bow. "Margaret."

Meg drew in a little breath, then turned and slipped from the room, leaving the two men alone.

James slung an arm around Graham's shoulder. "Port?"

If Graham had been dull when Meg was around, now he grinned and the man James had known nearly all his life returned. "I'd prefer scotch, truth be told."

"Scotch it is." James laughed as they made their way down the hall to the billiard room. Once inside, James moved to the sideboard to make the drinks.

"Since we're not rejoining Margaret, would you like a game?" Graham asked.

James nodded without looking at him. "We haven't played in an age."

He heard Graham placing the balls into position and turned to hand over a drink while Graham traded him for a cue. They each took a drink and set them aside before James said, "You first, mate."

Graham put himself into position and took his shot. As he did so, he said, "What's on your mind?"

James arched a brow. "On my mind?"

Graham straightened. "You have that look. I know that look."

James rolled his eyes. "You and Meg aren't married yet. Can't pull the concerned older brother act yet."

"Why not? I've been doing it over ten years already."

James half-grinned as he took his own shot, his ball striking both Graham's cue and the red ball. "Canon," he said softly.

"I saw it," Graham responded with a slight annoyance to his tone. He had always been competitive. It was why Simon didn't play with him anymore. "So what's the problem?"

James leaned his cue against the edge of the table and sighed. "Has Meg spoken much to you about this Emma Liston we were discussing at supper?"

Graham froze, leaning over the table for his shot. "In truth, Meg and I don't speak about much at all."

For a moment, James's focus on Emma faded and he stared at his friend. "Is there something wrong between you two?"

Graham took his shot, but he hit it too hard and it banked off the edge of the table and missed both his targets. He let out a low curse before he straightened up and glared at James.

"Of course not," he snapped. "Everything is fine."

"Fine," James repeated slowly.

Graham nodded. "Of course, we're planning a wedding, aren't we? And we've been friends for years. It's a good match, we both know it."

James wrinkled his brow. Neither Meg nor Graham seemed very pleased about their position, which wasn't what he'd ever intended when he suggested the engagement so very long ago.

"Graham—" he began.

"You asked about Miss Liston," Graham interrupted, turning his back so that it was clear the other subject was closed. "Why so interested in her?"

James pressed his lips together. For now, he would let the topic of the engagement go, but he made note to talk to Meg about it, for she might be more open. "She helped Meg and me with a...situation with Mother at the Rockford ball last week."

Graham turned and his eyes were now filled with concern. "A situation. Was she..."

James nodded. "Very. She's been having a rough go of it as of late. A few days ago at Meg's party and again tonight, which is why she didn't join us."

Graham shook his head slowly. There were few people who knew the full ramifications of Lady Abernathe's issues with drink. Graham was one of them, Simon another...and now Emma Liston.

Funny how Emma didn't seem out of place in that intimate list of his closest friends. Even though he hardly knew the girl at all.

"Emma Liston is a wallflower," Graham said, his voice becoming sharper, more business-like. "Her grandfather is a viscount. He and my father were cronies, which does nothing to recommend the man, as you know. *Her* father is estranged. A bad egg, as they say."

"I didn't ask you about her to get a listing of her family's every move," James said softly.

Graham shrugged. "It's what I do, remember things. I can't help it, so you might as well use it. Emma Liston is compromised."

"Compromised?" James repeated too loudly, rage bubbling up in him unexpectedly at the idea that some other man had touched Emma.

Graham stared at him. "Not *physically* compromised. I only mean she's in a bad position. Her dowry is small, the important members of her family do not acknowledge her and her father does nothing to add to her reputation."

James's heart rate slowly returned to normal. "Well, none of that means much to me."

"It should. The girl could benefit if she used anything she knows about your mother against you."

James shook his head, a flare of defensive anger rushing through him, even though he'd had the exact same concern about her the night of the Rockford ball. "I don't think so," he said. "She's made no secret of her position, nor has she made any attempt to leverage what she knows about my mother into a betterment of her position."

"Except she's now invited to your country party. A sought after invitation if ever there was one. People are always angling for me to get them one," Graham said with an arched brow.

"No, I don't think so," James insisted. "She's invited because Meg has fallen head over heels in friendship with her. And Emma hasn't been dishonest about her position."

"What do you mean?" Graham asked. "She told you about her wayward father?"

"No," James admitted, and was surprised by how his interest was aroused by that new information. "But she made it clear her position is precarious. She even made a joke about my pretending to court her to elevate that position."

"And you don't think *that* was angling?"

"No," James said through suddenly clenched teeth. "She was teasing, for God's sake. I never thought she meant it."

Graham stared at him, just stared, for what seemed like an eternity. "You want to do it," he finally said.

James drew back. "Do what?"

"Court her!" Graham said, throwing up his free hand in exasperation.

"I have no interest in courting her," James barked back. "I have no interest in courting anyone and you know it."

Graham's face softened and he said, "James—"

James held up a hand. "We're not discussing it," he snapped. "The point is that, yes, I *have* thought of Emma's statement. I have. Not because I actually want to court her, but because what she suggested, even half-heartedly, could very well help us both."

"I can see how it would help her—you're the most eligible bachelor in all of London. If you're seen paying her extra attention, men will circle. She'll suddenly be in fashion, just like the way you tie your cravat."

"I'm not sure it's fair to compare Miss Liston to a knot in a cravat," James muttered.

"To some there will be little difference," Graham said softly. "But I'm more interested in what you think this silly notion could do for *you.*"

"You saw how it was at the Rockford ball," James said. "It's the first event of the Season and they were already mobbing me. It was exhausting. And it will only get worse, you know. I've heard there's a large group of debutantes this year. Twice as large as last. They'll all be coming for me."

"And?"

"And if I am seen as interested in Miss Liston, they may pick another mark," James explained.

"And when she parts with you to, in theory, entertain a dozen true offers of marriage?" Graham asked.

James smiled. "I think I might be too broken-hearted to even dance this year after she's gone. Next might even be questionable."

Graham let out a sigh. "I am troubled by your attitude, my friend. But I am well aware there is no putting you off on a plan once you have it."

"Indeed, there is not," James said.

Graham shrugged and a boyish impishness he rarely showed anymore flashed across his face. "And it could be lucrative business for me, as well."

"How so?"

"Well, you've invited Simon and some of the others to this party, yes?"

James nodded. "Yes. Simon, Sheffield, Brighthollow and Roseford are attending. The others are busy and we haven't seen Willowby in years."

"Well, then we'll all be there to hear about your progress with Miss Liston. And place bets," Graham said with a chuckle as he returned his attention to their all-but-forgotten game.

"Place bets on what?" James asked as he lined up for his own shot.

"I don't know. If you'll fall in love with her and how quickly," Graham suggested as James took his shot.

The statement made James's hand slip and his ball actually hopped over the edge of the table and rolled across the floor. He scowled as he moved to catch it.

"If I decide to do this, no one is falling in love with anyone," he said with a laugh. "I can assure you of that fact."

Emma sat in the front parlor in the window seat, one leg tucked beneath her as the other dangled from the edge. She was watching the carriages drive by on the street. It was something she'd done since she was very young. She'd always wondered who was inside, where they were going, what they felt tucked into their little cocoons.

Today she wasn't thinking of those things. Her mind kept taking her to Abernathe. To those moments in the garden when he had been so unexpectedly kind. And she had been so stupidly candid.

The man didn't want to know her troubles. And he certainly didn't want to hear her ask him to court her, even in jest. He must think her an utter fool.

She certainly thought herself a fool.

"There you are." She looked toward the parlor door to find

her mother hustling in, a missive in her hand. "You have a message!"

Emma turned and slowly rose. Her mother must have pounced on the poor messenger the moment he came up the drive, for she hadn't heard the bell.

Of course, she hadn't exactly been attending, either.

She turned it over and recognized the seal. It was the same one that had been on her invitation to Meg's garden party a short few days before. It felt like a lifetime now.

Her hands shook as she broke it, and inside found a short letter from her new friend.

"Read it aloud!" her mother insisted, eyes bright with possibility and almost manic hope.

"Very well," Emma said softly. "'Dear Emma, I wanted to thank you again for your kind company after my party a few days ago. I truly treasure our talks. My brother and I are hosting a country gathering at our estate, Falcon's Landing. We would love to have your mother and you join us for the fortnight we spend there. I hope to receive your yes soon. With friendship, Meg.'"

As Emma read the words, Mrs. Liston had begun to clap her hands together and she was almost bouncing with delight as Emma lowered the letter. For her part, Emma was less excited. A fortnight at Falcon's Landing in the shire of Abernathe meant a fortnight with the duke, himself. A man who, she had already decided, thought her an idiot.

A man who made her nervous, and yet she found herself blabbering like a fool the moment he looked her way.

"Oh, Emma, you have made a good match in a friend," Mrs. Liston said, grabbing her arm and almost physically yanking her from her thoughts. "Lady Margaret! She is so very connected. You must use those connections."

"Mama," Emma said, pulling herself away and pacing across the room back to look out the window. "That is a mercenary way to look at a friendship."

"Well, we must be mercenary, mustn't we?" Mrs. Liston

said, her tone sharp enough that Emma turned to look at her. Her mother's hands were clasped before her, shaking. "You want to pretend that there isn't a rider pounding up behind us, bringing only destruction."

"That is a bit dramatic," Emma said softly. "We aren't trying to escape imminent death."

"No, it *isn't* dramatic. We're talking about the potential of societal death and you are old enough not to act like a child." Mrs. Liston folded her arms. "Tell me, Emma, how many times has your father swept back into our lives, dragging scandal behind him? How many times has he limited your options and humiliated me with his philandering and gambling and dueling? How many times?"

Emma tapped her foot. "You throw your anger and fear about Father up in my face any time I do not do as you ask, but we both know what will happen if he were to walk in that door tomorrow. You would open your arms to him, all would be forgiven and for a few weeks or months you would refuse to hear any negative opinion about him, no matter what he does."

Her mother's face crumpled at Emma's direct statement and her shoulders sagged. "You think me weak."

Emma held her breath, for there was not a good way to lie and deny her mother's charge. When it came to Harold Liston, Mrs. Liston was always torn between abject terror and blind devotion.

"It is complicated," Emma admitted at last.

"Yes, it is that," Mrs. Liston whispered, and her tears were real this time, not born entirely out of manipulation.

Emma sighed. She moved toward Mrs. Liston and caught her hands gently. "I do not dispute that you have reason to fear. Father *does* turn up at the most inopportune times and his behavior usually causes nothing but trouble."

"And he may very well show up yet again, you know," Mrs. Liston said with a sniffle. "It has been almost a year since we saw him last, and I wait to hear his footsteps almost every night now. Pounding up the stairs and dragging misfortune in his wake."

Emma bent her head. "I suppose that is possible."

"And this time I will not bend to his charms, I promise."

Emma pressed her lips together, for she knew that wasn't true.

"You know that if I am mercenary, it is because I am terrified that this time or the next time or the time after that he will bring something down on us that will destroy us permanently," Mrs. Liston whispered. "And the only way to avoid that fate is if you are married or at least engaged. Then he can blow and bluster, but his hurricane will not destroy us as it could now."

Emma reached into her pelisse pocket for a handkerchief. As she handed it over, she said, "I'm sorry I've failed you so far, Mama."

Mrs. Liston shrugged but didn't deny Emma's failure. "You have an opportunity here, my dear. And we are going to take it. We're going to that party."

Emma knew that tone. It was the one that brooked no refusal. She wouldn't convince her mother any differently no matter what she said.

"Very well, Mama," she said softly. "Though I cannot guarantee that I will leave this party with any more success than I have left any other."

Her mother's upset a moment before now seemed gone, replaced by grim determination on Emma's behalf. "You shall have ample opportunity to succeed. Surely there will be dozens of eligible men there for the pursuing, including the Duke of Abernathe, himself."

Emma's heart began to pound and she tried very hard not to think of dark eyes and the sadness within. Of big hands and broad shoulders. Of *him*.

She shook her head. "Abernathe is as interested in me as he is in a gnat, Mama," she said, but her voice sounded breathless and wavered slightly.

Mrs. Liston didn't seem to notice. "Then you should try

harder. You are not a great beauty, no, but you are not unattractive. If you didn't show your intelligence so much then perhaps you would have more luck."

Emma bit her tongue hard. Her mother had been saying that for years. It might be true that her mind brought her no suitors, but Emma didn't want a man who needed a stupid wife. She didn't want to hide who she was.

It was just that no one seemed to want who she was.

"I cannot force a man's attention," she whispered.

"So you will not even try? For me?" Mrs. Liston said, and then she began to cry fully.

Emma clenched her hands at her sides. *This* was manipulation and she knew it, but she couldn't help herself. She stepped forward and embraced her mother.

"Of course I'll—I'll try. We will go as you desire. And I will *try*."

Her mother gave a triumphant gasp and hugged Emma before she rushed from the room, calling for her maid and shouting about gowns and hats, like the outburst before had never happened at all.

After she was gone, Emma sank down into the closest chair and covered her face with her hands. Trying was one thing, succeeding was another. And in this moment, there didn't seem much chance of success at all.

CHAPTER SIX

One week later, James stood on the stairs at Falcon's Landing, watching the carriages pour into the drive one by one. At his side was his mother, who had managed to stay sober for the first time in weeks. And Meg stood at his other elbow, smiling and acting the true hostess of this soiree.

Normally he wouldn't have minded this duty. Many of those invited were his closest friends. Both Graham and Simon had ridden down to the estate with them three days before and the Dukes of Brighthollow, Roseford and Sheffield had already arrived. Their club wasn't complete, but he was surrounded by friends, regardless.

Yet James's mind was somewhere else as he shook hands and kissed knuckles and smiled at friends and acquaintances as they came up the stair and streamed into his home.

The duchess let out a long, put upon sigh at last and said, "Is that all, then?"

Meg began to speak, but James interrupted her as a final carriage turned into the drive. "No," he said softly. "There's one last one."

The carriage stopped and he found himself taking a step forward as one of his footmen rushed down to open the door for the occupants. Mrs. Liston exited first, in mid-sentence and her face flushed. He ignored her, leaning slightly to see Emma behind her.

She exited the carriage with a brief acknowledgment for James's servant and then stretched her back. She was wearing a blue gown. It wasn't anything fancy, not like some of the women who had stepped out in something fine to catch his eye. But the blue made Emma's eyes seem more cerulean. The green hue there faded slightly.

"James," Meg said, elbowing him in the side.

He blinked and found Mrs. Liston standing at the top of the steps, holding out her hand.

"Mrs. Liston," he choked out. "Lovely to see you, welcome to our home. You already know Margaret, I know."

Meg glared at him at his swift and dismissive welcome of the lady, and he heard her warmly making up for it with her own words as she introduced Mrs. Liston to their mother. James didn't care. He stepped closer as Emma mounted the last few steps and held out a hand to her.

"Miss Liston," he said.

She hesitated before she took his hand and let him help her to the landing. That hesitation was forever fascinating to him, for he'd never known another lady to be uncertain of him. But there was nothing reaching about Emma. Nothing grasping or false.

She didn't chase him.

"Your Grace," she breathed, then looked up at the house. "It is lovely."

He found himself watching her face for too long a beat before he turned to examine the house. "It is. This place has always been my escape. Perhaps later I could take you on a tour of it."

She jerked her gaze back to his face, and there was uncertainty in her expression. She didn't get to respond, though, for Meg caught her arm and pulled her into a hug. Emma's attention was taken then as the two young women began talking and laughing before Meg introduced Emma to their mother.

"Do you remember Miss Liston, Mother?" Meg asked when the formalities had been taken care of.

James watched the exchange carefully. Their mother had not had any recollection of her embarrassing display at the Rockford ball two weeks before. And she seemed to have no recognition of Emma as she stared blankly at her.

"I meet so many people," Her Grace said. "Liston, is it?"

Emma nodded, and there was no flash of judgment across her face, no response beyond one anyone would have when meeting someone for the first time. She smiled and held out a hand. "A pleasure to meet you, Your Grace."

Their butler, Grimble, appeared from the foyer and Meg squeezed Emma's shoulder briefly. "Go in, get settled. I'll come up later and we can have a real chat."

Emma nodded and then her gaze slid to James. She nodded slightly before her eyes darted away and she and her mother entered his home. He found himself catching his breath as she disappeared.

Meg turned toward him. "What is that expression?"

He blinked down at her. "Expression?"

Meg tilted her head. "Oh come, I know you too well. You look all...pinched. Do you not like Emma?"

He swallowed. "I think she's...fine. I don't really know her."

"Well, I like her," his sister insisted. "So *you* are going to have to like her, too. I think we could help her."

James pinched his lips together. Help her? Yes, he had his own ideas about that subject. Ones Meg might not exactly approve of. But he hadn't fully made a decision on that subject yet, so he merely nodded. "If she is your friend, she is my friend, I assure you."

"Is that everyone then?" the duchess asked, annoyance thick in her tone.

Meg gave James a meaningful look before she turned back. "Yes, Mother. Emma and her mother were our last guests. We can go in."

"Finally," their mother muttered as she trudged up the stairs away from her children.

Normally James would have been more focused on his mother and her behavior, but today his mind turned to other thoughts. Thoughts of Emma Liston. And they were far more pleasant than any worries about the duchess and whether or not she would cause a scene over the next two weeks.

Emma smiled at Sally as her maid folded the last item into her drawer and straightened up to say, "Is there anything else I can do, miss?"

Emma shook her head. "No, thank you. I think I'll rest a while. Grimble said supper would be at eight and I could use a moment."

Sally gave her an understanding look. Though Emma, of course, never spoke of her frustrations with her mother, Sally certainly saw and heard things. And two days crammed in a carriage together likely made Emma's difficulties clearer than usual.

"I'll come back at seven to help you change. Of course, ring for me earlier if you have a need," Sally said, then slipped to the door.

She opened it and let out a gasp that drew Emma's attention to the exit. Standing there was Meg, laughing as she raised a hand to her chest.

"I beg your pardon, my lady," Sally said, ducking her head.

Meg reached out and patted her arm. "Gracious, you frightened me. What good timing—were you just leaving Miss Liston to her own devices?"

"Yes, my lady."

"That leaves her all to me, then," Meg said, entering as Sally stepped aside.

Sally gave Emma one last questioning look and Emma nodded, excusing her. Sally shut the door behind herself and left Emma and Meg alone.

"I'm so happy you agreed to come," Meg said as she moved toward her and folded her into a warm embrace.

Emma hesitated a moment, but then squeezed her back. "I'm so thankful you invited me, my lady."

Meg pulled back and gave her a look. "Meg," she said with an arched brow.

"Of course, Meg," Emma said. "It will only take me a dozen times before I remember."

Meg smiled and looked around the room. "Is the chamber satisfactory?"

"Oh, indeed. I have a lovely view of the woods. I was…surprised that I wasn't sharing a room with my mother, though."

Meg grinned. "We are a full house and some of the ladies *are* sharing with sisters and mothers, but I made sure you had your own room. How else are we supposed to stay up until all hours of the night talking?"

Emma laughed. "Well planned then."

"James was pleased to see you again," Meg said as she moved to the window and adjusted the curtains slightly.

Emma tensed at that unexpected observation. "I'm certain he is pleased to have *everyone* invited here to visit."

"Not everyone," Meg said with a shake of her head. "He thinks I don't hear when he makes these little groans under his breath, but I do. He was reluctant about virtually every lady but you."

Emma felt her cheeks flaming. "He was happy because I was the last to arrive and he could go back to his friends."

Meg shrugged. "Perhaps."

"You and he are very close," Emma said, working to change the subject since this particular one made her very uncomfortable.

Now Meg's smile softened and her face lit up. "Oh, we are. He is three years older than I am, but has always included me."

Emma felt a fissure of jealousy at those words. She had grown up alone with a volatile father and a pushing, prodding mother. She'd often longed for a sibling to share her woes and her fun.

"It's hard to picture Abernathe as a child," she admitted. "He is such a...a man."

The moment she said the words, she clapped a hand over her mouth and stared at Meg. But Meg didn't seem to be offended by her overstep. In fact, she was laughing.

"He is a good pretender then," she said when she'd regained her composure. "For sometimes I look at him and all I see is that same little boy who used to walk tightropes and play matador with the bulls in the paddock."

Emma's eyes went wide at that image. "So he was always a daredevil?"

Meg nodded. "There was never a wager he didn't take. And somehow he always comes out unscathed."

"Some people are golden," Emma said with a shrug. "They never suffer."

Meg's laughter faded and her face became more serious. "Well, I wouldn't say that," she said softly.

There was something about her tone that made Emma cock her head in interest. The great Duke of Abernathe had suffered? The man who seemed to be able to do no wrong and led a gaggle of dukes? A gaggle seemed the best classification for a group of them.

It seemed unlikely. But then again, there was that hint of sadness in his eyes. The one she knew she wasn't supposed to see.

"Your brother has been kind to me," Emma admitted.

"Good," Meg replied with a sly smile. "Then you'll be happy to be sitting beside him at supper tonight."

Emma's eyes widened. "What? Oh Meg! You shouldn't have!"

Meg drew back. "Why ever not?"

"Because Abernathe is the host and he is terribly important. Having the seat beside his at supper is a place of prestige. Everyone will whisper if a person like *me* has that spot of honor."

Meg rolled her eyes. "You worry too much. And if people look and talk, isn't that a good thing? You *want* interest, don't you?"

Emma froze at that statement, so close to the very words she'd said to Abernathe in his garden in London not a week before. "Did...did Abernathe say something to you?"

"About what?" Meg asked, blinking in what appeared to be true confusion at the question and the sharpness with which it was asked.

"About me. My position," Emma breathed. She'd spilled out so many things to him in that day. And then she'd made her ridiculous joke about him courting her to gain favor. Her cheeks flamed just thinking about it.

"He didn't say anything to me," Meg said gently.

Emma let out a sigh of relief. At least her humiliation wasn't entirely complete. "Still, you shouldn't have arranged for such a thing, Meg. Truly."

"Your opposition is duly noted. Now I should go. I need to check on my mother and say a longer hello to a few other friends." Meg moved to the door and there she smiled. "Oh, and you should know that I didn't make the seating arrangements. *He* did."

Emma stared at her in mute shock as Meg left with a bright farewell. Then she sank down on the nearest chair. Abernathe had insisted she be seated beside him? That was unexpected news, indeed. As was the thrill that worked through her at the notion.

One she would have to tamp down entirely before supper began.

James leaned back in his seat, ignoring what was left of the supper on his plate. He looked to his left, to Emma. She was looking at her food, but she wasn't eating much, just pushing it around to make it look as if she'd eaten. But she was so focused on the act that it allowed him time to observe her.

In the week since she'd made her intriguing little joke about courting to garner attention, he'd done a bit of research into her and her family. What Graham had told him during their billiards game was just the beginning, for it was dark stuff. He found himself impressed by how little Emma reflected what she'd endured in either her words or actions.

But now he knew the truth and it made him examine her more closely. She wore fine gowns, not the finest, but definitely not inexpensive. And they had to take up a goodly amount of the funds she and her mother possessed, because he knew they had little money. Watching Emma, knowing how she felt about Society, he couldn't believe that was her choice.

Which meant she was being dragged forward to a life of her mother's choosing. Something he understood very well, if he replaced her mother with his father.

Emma was also known as something of a bluestocking. When the subject was broached, one gentleman had said something like "too smart for her own good or anyone else's". James supposed that was meant to put him off, but in truth it increased his interest. There was nothing he hated more than to spend time with some empty-headed chit. One who only mirrored his own opinions in some ridiculous attempt to get closer to him.

The one thing that no one talked about, which he noticed sitting next to her, was how pretty she was. Oh, she wasn't showy. She didn't try to be a diamond, not in word, action or look. But there was something about her that was undeniably attractive. And it wasn't just her stunning eyes and full lips. She was just…pretty.

He leaned forward and lowered his voice so only she would be able to hear him. "You know, that poor cow was killed once already, Emma."

She jerked her gaze to him, eyes suddenly wide as she

stammered, "I-I beg your pardon, Your Grace."

"I said the poor cow was already killed once and you are murdering it all over again by dragging it around your plate with that fork."

She looked down at the tracks she'd made in her food and then back up to him. And to his great surprise and utter triumph, she smiled. It was a broad, utterly honest expression, and for a moment he could hardly breathe. Her entire face lit up with it and there he saw the diamond she never allowed herself to be.

"I'm sorry," she whispered, completely oblivious to his thoughts. "The food is wonderful, I'm just..."

She trailed off and he cocked his head. "Just?"

She ducked her chin. "Nervous," she said so softly that he barely heard her.

"Why?" he pressed gently.

She lifted her gaze and met his, holding it there for a beat, then two. Until it became too long, until something heated flared low in his belly.

"Because of me?" he asked, his voice now rough.

She swallowed and he watched her delicate throat work with the action. "Yes," she murmured, her own tone much lower and huskier.

"Abernathe?"

He jolted at the sound of his name, said loudly from the other end of the table where Meg was holding court. He jerked his gaze to her and found that virtually every eye at the table was focused on him. On Emma.

Emma seemed to recognize it too in that moment and she blushed as she ducked her head a second time.

"Yes?" he said.

"I said perhaps it's time to end supper so everyone can ready for the ball." Meg lifted both eyebrows as she stared first at him, then at Emma.

"Excellent notion," he said, pushing to his feet. "Ladies and gentlemen, please join us in an hour in the ballroom."

The others began to rise, their talking filling the room as

they began to roam out in pairs or small groups. Emma took a long moment to stand and her hands shook as she placed her napkin on the table. James saw her mother waiting, attention focused entirely too closely on the pair of them. They only had a moment before she approached.

"Emma," he said, barely resisting the urge to take her hand. She glanced up at him. "Yes?"

"Will you walk with me in the garden?"

She blinked as if she didn't understand the question. "Walk with you? Now?"

He nodded. "There's an hour to the ball and I would have you back in time to get ready. Please, walk with me."

Her lips parted and she whispered, "Why—"

But before she could finish whatever she was going to say, her mother rushed up to them, her eyes lit up with frenzied pleasure. "Yes! Of course she'll walk with you, Your Grace."

James pursed his lips, for he didn't want Mrs. Liston's acquiescence. He wanted Emma's. Even though what he wished to discuss with her was little more than a business arrangement, he still wanted her...*surrender*.

A realization that put him a little off kilter.

"Is that a yes from *you*, Emma?" he asked.

She shot her mother a look and her cheeks were flame red as she nodded. "Of course, Your Grace. I would very much like that."

He wasn't certain if she was being honest with him in that statement, or just trying to appease her mother, who stood by them now, practically bouncing. Meg also stood near the exit, watching them with interest bright in her dark eyes.

In that moment, he didn't care. He was going to get his way. And as he took her arm and led her from the dining room, he felt a thrill of excitement he hadn't experienced for a long time.

CHAPTER SEVEN

Emma gripped her free hand at her side and tried to ignore the fact that her opposite one was locked around the Duke of Abernathe's bicep. His very muscular bicep. And he smelled good, too, damn him. Like cloves and leather. It was entirely unfair.

He guided her down the stairs, into the garden and through the winding pathway. They had not spoken since they left the dining room a few moments ago, and Emma finally pulled away from him and turned to face him on the path.

His face was lit by both the moon and a few lanterns that guided their way. In that soft half-light, she caught her breath. God, but he was all angles and curves. All hard maleness and it made her feel small and soft standing beside him.

But she didn't want to feel small and soft, because that meant vulnerable and foolish. She felt *that* quite enough already in this life she had so little control over.

She drew in a harsh breath and tried to forget that he was close and watching her with those intense eyes. She released his arm, placed her hands on her hips and snapped, "Why did you do that?"

He drew back in surprise at her tone and stared at her with exactly zero understanding on his face. "Do what?"

She huffed out a frustrated breath. "Make me sit by you at supper. Lean in and talk to me like we were discussing something intimate. Single me out to walk with you in the garden. Everyone was looking at us…at *me*, Abernathe."

His lips pressed together. "James."

She had more to say, but his soft admonishment brought her to a halt. "I beg your pardon? Did you just tell me that I should call you *James*?"

He nodded. "I would prefer it. I've never liked my title. It's a necessary evil to me."

She hesitated, for that statement made her wonder. Most dukes wore their title like a badge of honor, even though none of them had done anything to earn it except be a first son of someone else's first son. But Abernathe did truly look uncomfortable as he stood there.

And none of that had anything to do with her, yet here she was, pondering it. She scowled at him. "I cannot call the Duke of Abernathe by his Christian name. It would be wildly inappropriate."

"I call you Emma," he said with a slight smile.

"Yes, I've noticed that," she said, shivering at the way his lips formed her name. "And it is equally inappropriate, for I am an unmarried miss with no connection to you or to your family. All it does is place a false sense of—"

"You have a connection to my family," he interrupted, folding his arms and making his jacket strain back across his ridiculously broad chest. The one she couldn't stop staring at, even as she tried to admonish him for being too familiar.

"What connection?" she asked, fighting wildly for focus.

He arched a brow. "My sister adores you. You are her friend."

Emma stared at him, some of the fire going out of her at that statement. "Well, yes. Meg and I have become friends."

"Then what is the harm in me calling one of my sister's closest friends by her first name and her calling me by the same? Especially when we are in the privacy of a garden where no one else is around. It's not like I'm asking you to call me James in other places."

"So calling you James is a garden-specific request?" she asked, and then shook her head. What was she doing? Was she flirting with this man? This god? This golden child who didn't know the first thing about what it meant to be outside?

The very kind of man she had been avoiding her entire adult life?

He laughed, and the sound hit her right in the gut. Lower, actually. Significantly and inappropriately lower. Now she felt all...hot...and...and...tingly.

"*Privacy*-specific," he corrected. "When we are in private, I want you to call me James."

She shivered at the idea, foolish as it was. "*James*, do you really think we shall ever be in private with each other ever again?"

He looked at her closely and something in his gaze shifted. His lids narrowed and his pupils dilated as he stared at her. That hot and tingly feeling increased and she shifted, but her legs rubbing together only made it worse.

"Why not?" he asked softly.

There was a moment when she wanted to believe that a man like this could have any interest whatsoever in her. That he was different and could see past the issues that came along with courting her. That he could see past the intelligence that was a hindrance with so many men, that he could see past her lack of funds, that he could see past *everything* that made her unwanted.

But then reality returned and she glared at him.

"What are you doing?" she asked. "*Why* are you pretending that you could have any interest in me? What does it gain for you?"

"You are direct," he said with a shake of his head. "One more thing to like about you."

All her guards were raised now and she stepped back from him. "But *you* are not direct, Your Grace. Which makes me wonder what kind of game you are playing. Are you making sport with me?"

His lips parted as all humor and teasing went out of his

stare, his voice, his stance. "No," he said, almost in horror. "No, of course not. Why would you ask that?"

She flinched, a nerve exposed by his question, and it began to throb deep inside of her. She turned away from him. "You would not be the first, Your Grace. It doesn't matter."

She expected him to say something glib then. To find a way to escape the discomfort of this exchange. Instead she heard him move, she felt his presence just at her back. Her breath caught as his hand closed around her upper arm gently. He turned her and she stared up at him, so close that if she edged forward just an inch, she would be in his arms.

His fingers glided up her arm, across her shoulder, and then they brushed her cheek. She could hardly breathe as he took away that last inch between them. Her chest and thighs brushed his and she began to tremble.

"It does matter, Emma," he whispered. He was so close, his breath touched her lips.

She found herself lifting her chin, found her eyes fluttering closed as if some ancient instinct drove her to do so. And then his mouth brushed over hers and every thought, every hesitation, everything else in the world, faded from her mind.

His arms came around her and she gasped. He took advantage of her lips parting and traced his tongue across the opening. She froze. She'd never been kissed before—she had no idea what to do. But he didn't relent, he just tilted his head for better access.

And she gave it. Her body responded where her mind didn't know how and she opened to him, darting her own tongue out to touch his with hesitation. But hesitation soon gave way to other things. She lost herself in the sensation of his arms around her, his mouth on hers, his tongue brushing hers. It all made her come alive. Made her utterly aware of every flutter and tingle in her body…and in this moment there were plenty of them. It seemed she had found nerve endings where she never knew they existed and all of them throbbed in time to his kiss.

She clutched his arms and lifted into him, feeling her hips

bump his. He let out a strangled sound when she did that and then he drew himself away. She stood, dizzy, staring at him, and he stared right back, his breath short and his eyes wide.

Finally, she managed to find her voice and whispered, "Why—why did you do that?"

He blinked. "I didn't intend to," he said, just as soft as she had.

She frowned. The kiss had meant something to her and the idea that it had just been a mistake on his part was disheartening to say the least.

"Oh," she said.

"But I'm glad I did it," he continued, locking gazes with her. "Are you?"

She wanted desperately to deny him. To be able to say she didn't like it and walk away. To be able to pretend this man didn't move her. But she couldn't.

"Yes," she admitted. Heat filled her cheeks and she turned from him. "Oh, I should go inside. I should get ready."

"Wait, Emma!" he called out as she took a few steps away.

She froze, and slowly turned. God, he was devilishly handsome. Right now he looked so earnest, so driven.

"Yes?"

"I have a thought," he said. "A plan. It could help us both. That was why I wanted to talk to you out here tonight."

Disappointment she didn't want to feel filled her chest. In some small part of her she'd hoped he'd called her back for some more personal reason. Not a plan. Though what kind of plan that could be was completely unknown to her.

"A plan? I don't understand."

"You said something to me last week when we parted ways after Meg's garden party. It has stuck with me ever since," he said.

She took a step toward him as her mind turned back to their previous time alone together, in a different garden. She knew exactly what foolish things she'd said to him then. How she'd opened her soul to him the same way she'd opened her body a moment before. Somehow this man inspired that, as foolish as it was.

"What did I say?" she asked, faking innocence.

He arched a brow, his expression calling her on her faulty memory even if he didn't say a word about it. "When I asked if I could help, you said I could court you to make others notice you."

She gripped her fists and broke their intense stare. "Oh, please don't hold that silly thing over my head. I was just talking, I wasn't thinking. I didn't meant it and there's no need to—"

"It's a good idea," he interrupted. "The more I thought about it, the better it became. For both of us. If we courted, it would take every eye of every grasping mama off of me. And it would put every eye of every gentleman on you, just as you said."

She blinked. "So you want to…court me?"

He swallowed. "No. Well, not really. To pretend. To pay enough attention to you to garner interest without making irreversible promises. A tightrope, yes, but one we can walk if we are clear and careful."

Emma was shocked at the spreading pain in her chest that hit her as he explained himself. It wasn't as if she *wanted* to be courted by his man, kiss or no kiss. He was out of her league. By far.

"So you want to lie," she said.

He nodded. "A blunt way to put it, but yes."

"And how would that work, exactly?"

"Just like a normal courtship, except we know it isn't. We would dance together, we would flirt. I will say lovely things about you when anyone asks, you'll blush prettily when I'm mentioned." He grinned. "Yes, just like you're doing right now."

She lifted her hands to her hot cheeks. "Oh, Abernathe—"

"If we're plotting together, it really must be James," he said with an arched brow.

"But I'm not plotting, *you* are," she said. "I was only teasing when I said that to you last week."

"Were you?" he asked, suddenly serious again. "Be honest with yourself, *were* you teasing? I know a little about you, Emma."

Fear gripped her heart just as sadness had a moment before. "What do you know about me?"

He sighed, as if reluctant to say what he was about to say. "I know you've been out in Society for four years. I know you stand on the wall at parties, hating every moment. I know your mother is pressing at your back, demanding you save her."

"Save her?" Emma repeated, hating how her bottom lip trembled. Hating that he was right and could see everything that tormented her.

"Save her because the money will run out, especially at the rate she wants to spend it. And she puts all her hopes in you. It's a heavy burden, Emma, I can see it." His voice dropped and he took a small step toward her. "I *know* it. I'm offering to help you carry it. To give you a fresh chance you haven't had since you first came out."

She shook her head. "And you would do all this just to keep a few aggressive mamas away from you?"

He held her gaze for what felt like a very long time. She felt him reading her, analyzing what to do next. It seemed he'd made a decision when he said, "It's more than that. I suppose if I am to make demands, to ask you to be my partner in this, I must be honest with you. Emma, I don't want to get married."

"Ever?" she asked.

Slowly, he nodded his head, his gaze never leaving hers. "Ever."

She blinked. She'd heard those rumors, of course, that James was avoiding his duty. Meg had implied it, he'd said a few things about it, gossip screamed about it...but she'd assumed it was about putting the inevitable off for a year or two.

This was something else.

"Why?" she asked.

He froze, and discomfort crossed his handsome face. He stared off into the sky, lost to her as he pondered whatever troubles were on his mind. And there were troubles. She could see them moving across his face. Worse, she wanted to step forward and comfort him, even if it wasn't her place.

"It's complicated," he said at last, his face turning into shadow so she could no longer read it. "Suffice to say, I have my reasons. So will you help me? And be helped yourself in the process?"

She didn't answer right away. In that charged moment, she wanted to know so much more. To know why that sadness was in his eyes again. To know why he avoided his duty when it seemed he was a man of honor in his heart.

But he didn't want to show her those things and she had no right to ask for them.

"This is insanity," she said at last, for she had no other way to describe it.

To her surprise, he smiled. "You are here, Emma. We are in this situation already, aren't we? Why not help each other?"

She drew in a long breath. The world was currently spinning wildly out of control and she needed a moment before she agreed to anything so wild as his plan.

"Let me think about it," she said.

His eyes went wide, and for a moment it was like no woman had ever refused a request of his before. Perhaps they hadn't. He was a man who was hard to refuse.

Finally he nodded. "Very well, if that is what you require. Think all you'd like."

"I need to go up to the house. I need to…get ready, to just…to get ready."

"I can escort you," he suggested.

She looked at him, her lips still throbbing from where he'd kissed her, her knees shaking and shook her head. "No, I think you'd best stay here. I—oh, I'm just going to go."

She said nothing more and ignored him calling her name as she rushed from the garden and back up to the house. But being away from him didn't help as much as she'd hoped. Even as she fled his side, she still felt his gaze on her. His hands on her. His mouth on her.

And she still heard the words of his plan ringing in her ears as she went to get ready for what promised to be a very long night ahead.

CHAPTER EIGHT

James stared out across the ballroom floor and immediately caught sight of Emma. She was standing at the wall, just as she did at almost every ball or party she attended, but tonight she was not alone. Tonight a few gentlemen stood at her side, talking to her and Meg.

And while he should have been pleased with that—after all, it proved his point that his attention brought eyes and interest to her—instead it made his blood boil. Two of the men were idiots, couldn't rise to her intellect in any way. The other, Sir Archibald, was twenty years her senior, with two dead wives in his wake and eight truly rotten children.

"Why do you keep shifting around?" Simon asked, elbowing his side.

James blinked and broke his gaze away to refocus on Simon, Graham and another of their club, Robert, the Duke of Roseford. They were all staring at him, expectant and rather smug, if he read their expressions correctly.

"It's nothing," he grunted, turning his attention away from them.

Graham laughed. "Or is it Miss Emma Liston, who we all saw you talking with quite closely at supper?"

"Yes, and then the idiot goes for a walk alone with her in the garden," Roseford said, batting his eyelashes. "Careful, you'll have the lass in love with you and then what a pickle you'll be in."

James pressed his lips together at the teasing and ignored the flash of pleasure at the idea of Emma wanting him. "I'm not worried about that. I'm just shocked that she hasn't responded to my offer."

Graham lunged forward a step. "Your offer? Christ, James, don't tell me you went forward with that ridiculous idea you were telling me about in London."

"What idea?" Simon asked, looking between the two of them. "What is he talking about?"

James shifted in discomfort. He wanted his friends' advice, but not their taunting when the truth came out. "I thought Northfield would have told you all about it already," he said. "He had such a chuckle about it at my expense."

"Well, I thought you were in jest," Graham explained. "So I didn't say anything to anyone."

"What are they talking about?" Roseford asked, looking at Simon.

"Something I'm not privy to. Do either of you care to explain?"

Graham turned to them. "Before we left London, James came to me with this ridiculous notion that he would pretend to court Emma Liston to help her garner attention in the marriage mart—and to keep attention off himself." He glared at James. "Did you *really* approach her with this ridiculous plan?"

James folded his arms. "It isn't *that* ridiculous. I paid her the barest of attention tonight and look, she has men flocking to her side." He scowled as Emma smiled at something Sir Archibald was saying. "Though I do not approve the quality."

Roseford leaned forward, his dark eyes flashing with true emotion. "Have you lost your bloody mind? This is *exactly* how men get trapped into marriage with women."

Simon's expression was less harsh than Robert's, as was his tone. "So you actually talked to her about this?"

"In the garden before the ball," James admitted, his treacherous mind dragging him back to their kiss before he pushed the thought away. "She said she had to think about it. What is there to think about? I'm offering her something mutually beneficial. Why would she resist?"

Graham tilted his head back and began to laugh. "Great God, this is about her refusing you. You've *never* had a woman have the gall to say no to you."

James opened his mouth to refute that charge, but found he couldn't. He had always had ladies falling at his feet. They always danced with him, cooed over him, and if they were of a certain type, fell into bed with him.

Emma was different. In more ways than one. She'd kissed him back in the garden, yes. But there'd been no simpering and playing and flirting afterward. She'd hardly even acknowledged it happened. And here he was, still tasting her on his lips and feeling her in his arms.

It was madness.

"Correct me if I'm wrong, but haven't you declared multiple times before that marrying is not something you're interested in at all?" Roseford pressed.

James shifted. "Yes. And this ruse could very well help me further that goal. If I'm unavailable in the eyes of the mamas, they'll refocus their attention on others. And when Emma finds someone else, I will have a perfect excuse as to why I am not interested this Season or next or even the next after that."

Graham stared at him for far too long and the concern on his friend's face was clear. "If you don't want to marry, you could simply not marry. This convoluted plan isn't the best way to ensure it."

Simon was nodding, his own expression tight with worry. "And if you are truly concerned about Miss Liston, there are also easier ways to help her. There are a few in our group alone who are open to the idea of brides."

"You think I should arrange she meet with someone in our group?" James asked, his body going cold at the thought.

Roseford nodded. "Idlewood comes to mind. Christopher hasn't inherited his dukedom yet, but he's financially stable as

Earl, so her position might not be of difficulty to him."

A great wave of irritation swept through James as he looked at Emma and pictured her with their handsome friend. With *any* of his eligible friends.

"No," he said. "This is best."

Roseford let out a chuckle and said, "Well, if you insist. Now I see my mother signaling, so I shall be off."

Graham let out a long sigh. "I'll go with you. I should dance with Margaret."

James felt Simon stiffen at his side and shot his friend a look, but his face was unmoved. They said their goodbyes to their friends and were left alone. James continued to look out over the crowd at Emma.

As if she felt his gaze on her, she turned. Her face lost some of its color, then she whispered something to her companions, took a deep breath and began to move toward him. His heart stuttered as he watched her move through the sea of people.

Simon turned to him. "Looks like your answer is coming after all, James." He looked at Emma, then his attention moved off into the crowd. He shook his head slowly. "I'm not like Graham and Roseford. I don't know if what you're planning is right or wrong or just plain crazy. But I do know from bitter experience that if one doesn't take his opportunities, regret is a poor bedfellow. So do whatever you feel is right."

James glanced at him, troubled by Simon's long frown. But his friend didn't allow him to press on the issue. He merely patted James's forearm and then slipped away just before Emma reached him. Then all other thought emptied from his mind, leaving only her.

Emma could hardly breathe as she finished what felt like a very long walk from across the room. James was staring at her the entire way, which didn't help, for it was a very intense expression on his handsome, angular face. One that put her to mind of the garden and his unexpected and highly pleasurable kiss.

She stopped before him, shoving her shaking hands behind her back. "Your—Your Grace," she said softly.

He tilted his head, examining her closely before he said, "Would you like to dance, Emma?"

She jolted at the suggestion. Somehow she hadn't been expecting it. But there was no avoiding it, so she nodded. He held out a hand and she took it, electricity racing up her arm that she tried hard to ignore. She felt every eye in the ballroom turn toward her as he guided her to the dancefloor. As the music began, she held back a groan.

A waltz. Of course it would be a waltz. Anything to force her to remain in his arms like she belonged there, when she most certainly did not.

He placed a hand on her hip and spun her into the first steps. She found herself staring up into his face, perfectly guided by him. He was everything a man should be when he danced. He was lithe and graceful, but he led with a firm hand, turning her exactly where he wanted her to go.

He smiled down at her. "It would probably help if you looked slightly less terrified, Emma. People will think I'm holding you hostage."

She couldn't help but laugh at his light tone. It drained some of the tension from her body and made her steps easier. She drew in a long breath. "If I look nervous, it is because I've been thinking about what you suggested in the garden."

His fingers tightened against her back, drawing her just the tiniest fraction closer. "Have you? And what did you determine your answer to my plan to be?"

"It is madness to participate in such a deception," she said, watching a flash of emotion cross his face before he went back to calm and unreadable. "But..."

"But?" he pressed.

"I have almost nothing to lose with the effort," she

admitted. "So if your offer still stands, I will agree to the terms."

He smiled, an expression that lit up his face and made her stumble in her steps. Great Lord, but he was beautiful. Truly beautiful, like some kind of wicked angel.

He steadied her as he said, "My dear, we have not yet come to terms."

She wrinkled her brow. "Haven't we? I'm agreeing to your ruse."

He spun her deftly as he said, "But there are details. And details are incredibly important, especially in an arrangement like this. But here on the dancefloor with the world watching is not the place to hash those out."

She glanced around and drew in a sharp breath. Indeed, the world did seem to be watching. Women were glaring at her over their fans, gentlemen were talking and sizing her up. She shifted with discomfort, for she had never been the center of such attention before.

"Where then?" she asked, her voice catching.

He pondered the question a moment. "My sister says she has provided you with a room to yourself?"

Her lips parted. "You cannot mean to come to my room, Your Grace."

There was a dark flare of heat in his eyes, but then he shook his head. "No. I think that would not be a wise idea, considering."

"Considering what?" she asked on the barest of breaths.

He shrugged, but once again his fingers slid along her spine with an intimacy that made her shiver. "Just considering. I only mentioned it because if you are alone, it will make it easier for you to sneak out. Will you join me in the library in a few hours?"

She considered the question a moment. Sneaking out of her chamber in the middle of the night to rendezvous with a scandalous, highly sought after and incredibly attractive man did not seem like the most proper thing to do. But then again, she had been behaving properly her entire life and what had it gotten her?

Impropriety was beginning to look like it had its perks.

She nodded. "I will."

He smiled at her again as the music ended. "I look forward to it, Miss Liston," he said with a formal bow.

She executed her own curtsey. "Thank you, Your Grace."

He took her hand and led her from the dancefloor. But before he released her, he bent and pressed a kiss to her gloved hand. The warmth of his breath pierced the thin fabric, swirling around her skin until her thighs clenched together.

He nodded and let her go, trailing off into the crowd as if he had no care in the world. And perhaps he didn't. After all, this little ruse of his likely meant nothing to him, just as their kiss earlier meant nothing to him.

And she had to make sure she was just as cool about it or else she would put herself in a world of trouble.

Emma came down the long staircase hours later, peering around through the now-shadowy halls for fear of being caught. She had hatched an elaborate explanation while she waited for the proper time to come downstairs. One that involved an inability to sleep, a love of libraries and a need for a boring book.

She could only hope she'd never be asked to recite it, for she wasn't very good at lying.

She huffed out a breath as she muttered, "Exactly why you're entering into a ruse of a courtship with a...a..."

She pushed open the library door and caught her breath. James was already there, standing by the fire. He had shed his jacket and his cravat, and his shirt was open two buttons, revealing a smooth line of chest that made her blush. As she stumbled into the room, he looked up at her, heat swirling in his dark eyes as he looked her up and down.

"...scoundrel," she finished.

He blinked. "I'm sorry?"

She shook her head. "Oh—I—nothing. I was just…nothing."

"Close the door, will you?" he asked.

She looked behind her at the door. Her only remaining bastion against whatever might happen once they were alone. She turned back and found he had taken a step toward her.

"If we're going to have a private conversation, it would be best," he said, his tone soothing. Hypnotic, almost. She found herself reaching back and doing as he'd asked.

When the door clicked behind her, she leaned against it. "I-I'm sorry I'm late," she said, searching for normalcy. For calm. "I had to redress myself and it took longer than I thought it would."

He moved closer and suddenly she felt his heat. In the dim library, in the quiet, in the private where no one knew they were together, everything felt close and intimate. She swallowed hard as she looked up into his face.

"I'm glad you came," he said, his voice rough.

She felt off kilter so close to him, so she stepped around him into the room and looked around. "Oh, it's beautiful," she breathed as she peered up at the high bookshelves lined with books in spines of rainbow colors. They seemed to stretch forever.

"I agree," he said, his presence right at her back again. "I have always loved this room."

"Have you read all the books?" she teased as she looked at him over her shoulder.

She expected him to wave off the idea of sitting to read for hours, but he instead looked up at the shelves. "Almost," he said. "There are still some tomes on minute farming techniques that are slow reading, indeed."

She spun around to face him. "You must be joking. You really read all these books? You?"

He arched a brow. "Did you believe I couldn't read? My professors would be very cross."

She shook her head. "Of course I thought you *could* read. I just never pictured a man like you as wanting to beyond a daily paper and perhaps a pamphlet on horse races."

"A man like me," he repeated. "What sort of ideas do you have about me, Emma Liston?"

She pressed her lips together. Now that she'd bumbled out such foolishness out loud, she didn't want to say more. Not with him standing so close.

"I don't know," she said.

"Yes you do. Go on, tell me." He folded his arms, eyebrows lifted, waiting.

She huffed out her breath. "I suppose I have always seen you as a...golden child. You can do no wrong, everyone loves you, you've never had to work for anything. Obviously you are a decent sort or you wouldn't have such leeway, but I admit you never struck me as a...studious person."

"A golden child who never had to work for anything," he repeated. "You almost couldn't have gotten it more wrong." He smiled, but it wasn't like his earlier expressions at the ball. This was tight and humorless. Pained.

"I'm...sorry," she said softly. "I do not like to be judged by others and I see that I did just that to you. It wasn't fair."

His expression softened a fraction and he reached out to take her hand. Neither of them wore gloves, so just like in the garden his skin brushed hers, and she barely held back a shuddering sigh of pleasure at the sensation.

"Apology accepted," he said softly. "And I hope you'll find I'm full of surprises the longer we know each other."

He was leaning closer now and her heart began to pound. She felt hot and cold all at once. This was out of control.

She jerked back a step and stammered, "T-terms. We were meant to discuss terms of our agreement. What were they?"

He watched her for a beat and then nodded. "Quite right. Straight to business." He motioned toward two chairs set toward the fire. She took one, smoothing her skirts around her reflexively as she watched him take his own.

"What did you have in mind?" she asked.

He glanced at her. "We'll have to be careful, of course. Our courtship cannot seem too serious or else it will serve neither of us. But we will chat in front of others, flirtation is the name of the game."

She shifted. "I'm afraid I'm not very well versed in flirtation."

He leaned in. "No? Why is that?"

"I-I've never had need for it, I suppose. No one ever...wanted me."

"I very much doubt that," he said, a gravelly tone to his voice that made her toes curl in her slippers. "But flirtation is not difficult. You smile, you laugh, perhaps you make an effort to touch me."

"Touch you?" she repeated, her errant mind flying back to their earlier kiss.

"Not intimately," he said slowly. "I meant a touch on the arm. On the hand. While we're talking."

She shivered. "I can...try."

"Touching me makes you nervous?" he asked.

She felt blood rushing to her cheeks and reached up to cover them with her cool hands. "Yes," she admitted when it was clear he expected an answer. "Yes, it makes me nervous."

"Why?" he asked.

She bent her head. So many inappropriate answers swirled through her mind. None of them were something she could say out loud. Not to him. God, not to anyone.

He slid forward on his chair and reached out. He touched her chin and forced her to look at him. "Are you nervous because we kissed?"

She nodded. "No one has ever...done that before. And I...I just..."

His lips pressed together and he looked displeased. Her heart leapt. Probably she had entirely mucked this up. He would think her an idiot now and walk away. That was probably for the best, despite how he believed he could help her. But for the best or not, she found she didn't want him to reject her.

"You are so innocent," he said softly. "So sheltered."

She blinked as he slowly dropped to his knees on the fancy rug before the fire and inched over to her. He was so tall that even up on his knees he was even with her face as she sat in the chair. He moved in, placing one hand on either armrest, and lifted up.

Their lips were now a hair apart and she began to shake. "What are you doing?"

"Perhaps you need help in more than just garnering attention," he whispered. "Fear is a killer, Emma. It will destroy what you want faster than any other thing. I don't want you to be afraid of me. Of the unknown. Of…this…"

He braced up, and his lips brushed hers for the second time in just a few hours. It was less surprising to her now. She found her arms folding around his neck and her mouth opening to him. He leaned in, and she met him halfway, tangling her tongue with his as he pressed her back in the chair and kissed her like he was a starving man and she was all the food in the world.

"You're a natural," he groaned against her mouth. "Made for pleasure."

She didn't really understand what he meant, but she shivered at his words nonetheless. Pleasure—oh, there was so much of that. She ached for more in the most outrageous places. Like in her hard nipples, low in her stomach, between her legs.

He drew back and met her stare. His was wide and a bit wild. Like he was battling a beast within himself. One that wanted something she didn't truly understand, but she found herself leaning toward him. Toward it.

She caught the back of his neck and drew him to her, brushing her lips to his. He made a harsh sound in his throat and then he devoured her, pinning her to the chair as he crushed her hard against him and spiraled her into surrender once more.

CHAPTER NINE

James pressed hard against Emma's softness, her quiet mewls of pleasure stoking a fire in him that he hadn't felt in…well, a very long time. He was no monk—he took his pleasure and had had mistresses over the years. None had ever inspired such lust as that which burned in him now. And he had no idea why.

Was it because Emma was so innocent? Because she was so different from the women he normally pursued? He had no idea, but he burned to touch her, to brand her, to take her.

But there could be none of that. Fake courtships and stolen kisses were one thing. Once he breached her, there would be no going back. Of course, that didn't mean they couldn't find pleasure.

He leaned back and looked into her face. Her eyes were shut, her lips shiny and full, her breath short as she panted beneath him. Oh, how he wanted to make her shatter. To wake her to a world he doubted she'd ever imagined.

"I want to touch you, Emma," he whispered.

Her eyes flew open, and the blue-green was so soft and beautiful as she stared up at him through the dark. "Touch me? Aren't you already touching me?"

He held back a groan. God damn but that sweetness, that innocence, was like catnip to him. His need to make her come multiplied.

"Not like I want to be," he said, his voice harsh in the quiet. "I want to touch you...here."

As he said the words he dragged his hand down her body and pressed between her legs, gathering the fabric of her gown there. She hissed out a sound of surprise and lifted her hips against him.

"I don't...I haven't...I want..."

"What do you want?" he asked.

She shook her head. "I don't know." Her gaze snagged his, wide and wild. "I don't know, James. I just feel...full. Like I'm going to burst."

"I can make it better," he assured her as he caught the edge of her skirt and pushed it up. He held her gaze as he did it, watching her. He would stop if he had to. If she wanted him to. No matter how impossible that seemed.

But she didn't ask. She just stared at his ever-rising hand lifting her skirt inch by inch. He slipped his fingers beneath the hem when he got it to her knees and touched her bare legs.

"James!" she cried out, her hands coming to cover his through her skirt.

"I can make it better," he repeated as he leaned in and kissed her again.

She sank back, her hands drawing him close, her tongue tangling with his. He slid his hand up over her knee, to her naked thighs, and finally he found her drawers. They were silky and soft, but he wanted something better to touch. Something sweeter.

He found the narrow slit in the fabric and parted it, pushing his hand in to where she was exquisitely hot and already wet. He could feel that wetness on her thighs.

He pulled away from the kiss and stared down at her as he smoothed his fingers across her entrance. She shivered at the touch and stared up at him with wild eyes.

"This won't ruin you," he promised, though in his heart that was exactly what he wanted to do. He wanted to spread her legs wide and slide inside of her, he wanted to claim her until she trembled beneath him, until he found his fill of her.

But that wasn't right. Neither was what he was doing at present, but at least it wouldn't destroy her.

He pressed her outer folds open, his fingers slipping along her slick entrance. She moaned out a soft sound of pleasure as her hips jolted up against him and forced his fingers across her once again.

"What is this?" she whispered, her cheeks flaming.

"Pleasure," he managed to ground out past clenched teeth. "This is pleasure, Emma."

He smoothed his fingers along her again and again, then pressed lightly on her clitoris. She dug her fingernails into the chair arms, her eyes widening as she gasped out his name.

Hearing it said in pleasure was almost enough to take him over the edge. He leaned in and kissed her again, sucking her tongue as he worked at her, drawing her to lift against him, to find the release he could feel trembling through her.

And at last she found it. He felt her body tense against him as she cried out softly. Her hips lifted, her body thrashed and she gave over her orgasm in quick, focused waves.

When she had come through the crisis, he withdrew his hand from her, sliding her skirts down properly as he reluctantly got to his feet and stepped away from her.

She stood immediately, her face pale and her eyes wide as she stared at him. Her lips parted and closed, and he could see her fighting with something to say. But before she could do it, the door to the library swung open.

They both turned toward it and watched as the Duke of Sheffield entered the room. As Baldwin saw them standing together in the middle of the library, in the middle of the night, he came to a sharp halt.

"I beg your pardon," he said, his gaze sliding to James in question. "I didn't realize anyone else was up at this hour."

Emma said nothing—she just gave James a horrified look and fled the room, her cheeks flaming and her steps unsteady as she flew past Sheffield without so much as a side glance. James watched her go, wanting so much to reach out to her, to tell her it was all right, that she hadn't done anything wrong. But he couldn't.

He glared at Sheffield as he softly shut the door behind him. "Good timing."

Sheffield threw up his hands. "I apologize. Though I'm not sure how I was to know you were in the library with…" He glanced over his shoulder. "With Emma Liston."

James rubbed a hand over his face. "By the way you say her name, I assume Roseford, Simon and Graham have told you all about my plans with her."

"Such gossip is bound to travel fast in our group, especially if we're all under one roof. Brighthollow and I had a long talk about it with Roseford earlier today."

"God," James muttered, rolling his head back. "And what did the rooster society decide?"

"That you're an idiot to come up with such a plan," Sheffield laughed. "But you know Brighthollow and Roseford are both incredibly opposed to marriage. Probably more than even you are. So they aren't the best judges of what is right."

James looked at Sheffield. He'd always liked Baldwin. Of their group, he was the quietest, the one who kept his problems close to the vest. Simon and Graham were so close to James, and Baldwin was right that Roseford and Brighthollow were the least likely to give him any advice except to run screaming from Emma lest he get caught in some kind of trap.

But in this moment, he needed advice. Good advice from someone less involved and less biased. Because what had happened a few moments before with Emma was entirely out of control. It hadn't had a damn thing to do with a plan or helping her or helping himself. He'd just wanted to touch her, and he'd done so without a thought to the consequences or the rules or anything except how he wanted to see her face when she came.

She had not disappointed. Her release had been powerful and erotic and infinitely sweet. But it muddied the waters of his plan a great deal.

"I don't know what I want from her," he admitted softly.

Sheffield hesitated a moment, then moved forward to motion him to sit. Once they both had, he leaned forward, draping his forearms over his knees, his face intense with concern and focused. "I thought this false courtship you've proposed was just a ruse to help you both. Though I certainly got a sense there was more going on between you when I entered the library."

James shook his head. "I...she isn't the kind of woman who normally catches my eye, and yet there is something about her that draws me in. Tonight I...I may have gone a bit too far."

"How far?" Sheffield asked softly.

"Not so far as to ruin her, too far to be gentlemanly," he said slowly. "I know I can tell you this and not have you say anything."

"I won't say a word to anyone," Sheffield reassured him. "Though I admit I'm surprised. You have never made a move that didn't seem calculated."

"I'm not sure that's a compliment," James said. "But I'm also not certain it is wrong. Though I know my reputation can be a bit wild, I do actually think through most of my actions. Especially the ones that will affect others. Tonight, I didn't think. And perhaps that means I should back away from Emma. For both our sakes."

He said those words and his chest hurt with the thought. He pushed to his feet and walked away from his friend to the window, where he stared out at the darkness with unseeing eyes.

"What has changed since you first came up with this idea to help her?" Sheffield asked after a few seconds of silence had passed.

James turned back. "What do you mean?"

"I mean, has Miss Liston's position increased in any way?"

James shrugged. "The little bit of extra attention I've paid toward her so far has seemed to help her a bit, but no. She is still in the same position."

"And has her family come into more money or any other

thing that might give her more value in the eyes of some?" Sheffield pressed.

"No, of course not," James said. "What are you getting at?"

"We both know that this plan of yours is more beneficial to Miss Liston than it is to you." Sheffield folded his arms across his chest. "You may pretend not to care, but I recognize that you want to help her. And that is not the worst impulse. Many people have…" He hesitated. "Have things that happen that are not in their control. Things that damage them. And good people *should* help. So if you are asking me what I think you should do, I think helping the young woman is still the right thing to do."

James stared at Sheffield. No one had spoken to him about his plan in those terms. If he abandoned Emma now, just because he was uncomfortable with the desire she inspired in him, was it being fair to her? After all, he had dragged her into this idea. She never would have asked to be in this position without his prodding.

"I know you are right," he said at last.

Sheffield smiled, and there was some relief to his expression. As if he were truly invested in the idea of James helping Emma. James looked at his friend more closely.

"Why are you up so late?" he asked.

Sheffield shifted. "I couldn't sleep," he said. "And I thought a book might help."

James frowned. "You've been of great help to me tonight. Can I be of some to you?"

Sheffield held his gaze for a moment and then he shook his head. "No, my friend, I think not. Thank you for the offer, though. I do appreciate it." He pushed to his feet. "I'll be off to bed now. You should do the same. It seems you have some damage to repair with Miss Liston tomorrow. I hope you will make it clear to her that I have no intention of speaking to anyone about finding you two in the library tonight."

"I will," James said, holding out a hand to Sheffield. They shook. "Thank you."

Sheffield shrugged. "You're welcome," he said. "Good

night."

He left the room then, leaving James to stand and stare at the flames dancing in the fire. Tonight he had gone too far with Emma and he should have felt sorry for it. He didn't. In fact, all he felt was a stronger urge to do it again. To do more.

And all he could do was try to control that part of him that wanted to take and claim her. To focus on the true matters at hand and not let Emma Liston's unexpected charms veer him from his course.

CHAPTER TEN

If Emma had hoped that a good night's sleep would help, that was not to be. First because sleep had not come at all, second because no amount of time or space could change what she had done with James in the library.

Now she sat at the breakfast room table, staring at her plate, reliving every heated, passionate moment between them. Could the others see it on her face? Would the Duke of Sheffield tell anyone about their encounter?

She had no idea, but she trembled at it and the knowledge of what either of those things could do to her. And in truth, she trembled at her memories too. Wrong or not, what James had done to her when he touched her was nothing short of magnificent. She'd never felt such pleasure. Even now her toes curled when she thought of it.

It was all very confusing.

As if the universe sensed her confusion, James came through the breakfast room door at that moment. She made a soft, strangled sound in her throat as he paused, his dark gaze sweeping over the room until he found her. Their eyes locked, and in the depths of his smoky stare she saw passion and heat and promises that would never be fulfilled.

She turned her face to break the eye contact and focused on

slowing her breathing as best she could. To no avail.

"Good morning," James said to those who were already awake and eating. It was not their entire party, that was certain. Only about half those in attendance were downstairs, but those who were called out greetings.

James strode through the room and plopped himself in the seat across from Emma. She felt the eyes of the ladies track to her, and blushed as she glared at him.

"Don't," she said through clenched teeth. "Don't."

His expression softened as stared into her eyes, concern written across every line of his handsome face. "Emma," he said softly.

"Your Grace," she said back, sending him a look to remind him they were in public now, not a private garden or on the dancefloor or in a…library.

He pressed his lips together hard and glanced up at the servant who brought him coffee and a plate of food. Once they were alone again, he leaned in closer. "I want to talk to you."

She shook her head slightly. "Here?"

"No," he said. "Too many people. Excuse yourself and meet me on the terrace off the parlor across the hall."

"Everyone will watch us leave together."

"Isn't that the plan?" he asked.

She sighed. The plan. God's teeth, after last night she'd all but forgotten his plan. His plan to find her some other man to marry, a man who wouldn't know that the Duke of Abernathe had put his hands up her skirt and made her world turn to rainbow colors and intense waves of unimaginable pleasure.

Damn him.

"Fine," she said, pushing aside her half-empty plate.

She rose and departed the room with just a few words here and there to those in attendance. Thank God her mother and Meg both weren't up yet. Emma was quite certain each of them would notice the odd interaction between Emma and James. Meg because was too sharp not to. Mrs. Liston because she was obsessed with every move Emma made when it came to the prospects of a duke.

She stalked across the hall, into the parlor and out the French doors onto the terrace. The late spring morning sun hit her face and she drew in a long breath of fresh country air. Her heart rate began to slow as she did so. Her hands stopped shaking and for the first time since last night, her wild mind calmed and let her think clearly.

But all she could do was think of James touching her. Of her body doing things she had never imagined were possible. Things she'd liked, if she were honest with herself.

All her life, she had been forced into situations she didn't enjoy. She'd been forced to be afraid thanks to her father's antics. Forced to dance when she did not wish to. Forced to pretend that rejection didn't hurt. Forced to hide her intelligence.

But last night it was if the chains of all those things, all those situations, had been lifted from her and she'd flown beneath his hands. Spiraling up to the sky until she feared she'd burn in the sun. And it had felt damned good.

"Emma?"

She jumped at James saying her name and turned to find him closing the terrace doors. He moved toward her, hesitating, his expression uncertain. Her heart sank at the sight. He must regret what they did, especially since his friend had seen them together in what would be a compromising position by any definition.

"Good morning," she said with a sigh.

He tilted his head. "Are you...well?"

"If you are asking if I slept well, I did not," she said, looking away from him so he wouldn't see her blush.

"I admit neither did I," he said, his tone almost relieved. "I-I couldn't stop thinking about the library, Emma."

She dared to look at him and found him focused so intently on her that it felt like he imprisoned her with his stare. Her lips parted and she took a half step toward him. "I have also thought of it a great deal since last night."

"What I did...what I did was ungentlemanly, Emma," he

said. "And dangerous."

"Your friend…the Duke of Sheffield—" she began, but he cut her off.

"Baldwin will not say a word, I vow that to you. He is a good man, he has no desire to hurt either of us," he said. "Our secret is safe with him."

She let out a short breath of relief. "And yet you still regret what you…*did*?" she asked, hating to hear the answer but knowing she needed to hear it. Only the truth would wake her from this dream that somehow this man really wanted her.

He swallowed hard before he spoke. "That is not what I said, Emma. I said what I did was wrong. I did not say I regretted it."

She gasped and shook her head. "What do you mean?"

"I wanted you," he whispered. "And that wanting took over my reason, which was wrong. I put you in a situation where you could have been damaged greatly by my actions. But as far as touching you went, as far as making you come…that was a pleasure."

"You liked it?" she asked, shocked.

He nodded slowly. "Very much. But I know I must apologize because I am far more experienced than you are. I never should have coerced you into allowing me such liberties, no matter how strong my desire for you was."

She moved forward again, and now they were dangerously close. Not quite inappropriately, but edging toward it. And she didn't give a damn.

"James," she whispered, breathless. "What happened last night…that was the first time I have felt alive in…in a very long time. I didn't even know it was possible to feel like you made me feel."

He lifted a hand, and in that moment everything slowed. He clearly wanted to touch her and she so desperately wanted him to do just that. But then his gaze slid to the door and he lowered his hand with a frown.

"I'm glad you don't regret it," he said softly.

Relief flowed through her, as well as desire she was starting to understand. "Could we…do it again?"

She couldn't believe how daring she was being, and from the way his eyes went wide, he also was surprised by her boldness. "You want to?"

She nodded. "James, even if your grand plan plays out just as you hope and some man takes an interest in me and asks for my hand, in my heart I'll always know he wanted me only because he felt he was taking something from you. I have little choice in what my future will be, thanks to my circumstances, but if I could go into that future with more memories of…" She shivered. "What we did, I would like it."

His frown deepened, and she thought for a moment that he might refuse her. But at last he sighed. "Very well, we can make it a term of our agreement. We will continue our pretended courtship, just as we decided last night. If we have the chance to find a bit of pleasure like last night, we will." He leaned in. "And I vow not to ruin you, Emma, no matter how difficult that promise may be to keep."

She held out a hand. "That is a bargain, Your Grace."

He smiled at the offering and took it, but instead of shaking on it, he lifted it to his lips and pressed a kiss to the top of her glove. "A bargain," he said. "Now we should rejoin the others. Margaret has a whirlwind day planned, I believe, including a rousing game of Pall Mall on the west lawn and a picnic by the stream. All of which will allow us ample opportunity to enact the first part of our plan, if not the second."

She smiled, for the lightness had come back into his tone and his face, but beneath her smile there was a stir of wanting. She'd been reluctant to come here, but now her entire life had been set on its head by James, his plan and his touch.

She could only hope she could maintain some kind of control over herself and her emotions, lest she begin to believe there could be something more between them than a ruse and a few stolen moments of pleasure.

James couldn't help but grin as he watched Emma and Margaret from across the wide lawn. In the midst of the Pall Mall game, the two were laughing riotously as Emma tried to set up a winning shot and failed miserably. She bent at the waist, her entire body shaking with mirth.

And she was glorious. Lit up like a thousand candles lived within her, flushed just like she'd been beneath his hands the night before, relaxed and at ease like she belonged here. With him.

How anyone could see her as she was in that moment and not want to be near her was beyond his comprehension. He certainly wished to cross the distance between them, swing her around by the waist, press a kiss to her full lips until she went limp in his arms.

"Interesting little creature, isn't she?"

James stiffened as Sir Archibald approached, a drink in his hand and a leer on his round, sweaty face.

"I'm certain I don't know who you mean, Sir Archibald," James said, his tone cool.

He'd never liked the man, but he lived in James's shire and had always ingratiated himself to James's father and later to him. But James found him a pompous windbag who ate and drank too much.

The fact that he'd been hanging around Emma earlier in the party only made James's disdain all the more focused.

"Don't you?" Sir Archibald said with a chuckle. "I thought I'd seen you sniffing around Miss Liston, was I wrong?"

James let out a long, deep breath. "She's a good friend of Margaret's," he explained, then thought of their plan. He'd promised Emma he would infer his interest to garner that of others. He hadn't exactly been thinking of someone like Sir Archibald, but what could he do? "And I like her."

Archibald smiled broadly at that admission. "She isn't

exactly a great beauty, eh? But there's something about her. Something with a little fire to her. I might throw my hand in there for her, myself. It's not as if she has many prospects, does she?"

James felt his nostrils flaring. Sir Archibald had insulted Emma not once but twice in the span of five sentences, and James now wanted to do nothing less than slam a fist through his face. Instead, he gripped his drink harder and said, "She may have more prospects than you think. And isn't she a bit young for you?"

"The younger the better," Sir Archibald laughed with a friendly nudge to James. "But you could have anyone, Abernathe. For God's sake, don't drop yourself low. Your father would have wanted you to wed someone of importance, someone to increase your name."

James gritted his teeth. Yes, his father would have wanted him to do a great many things. Exactly why James had no plans of doing them. "If you consider Miss Liston so low, why would *you* consider her?"

"Well, as you said, I'm an old man," Sir Archibald chuckled. "My heirs and spares are already older than you are, the ones who aren't could use a woman around to deal with them. I don't need to raise myself through a marriage. I just want a young chippy to spread her—"

"Enough," James said, turning on him with what he knew was a dangerous look. "You shall not speak of Emma in such a fashion. Not here, not to me nor to any other guest."

Sir Archibald's face fell and there was a flash of anger in his eyes before he held up his hands. "Coming to the girl's aid, are you? Well, before you throw yourself headlong into some kind of arrangement with her, you'd best do a bit of research on her. And her father."

James folded his arms. "I know about her father."

It was a half-truth, of course. He knew the man had been cut off from his family, that he was not around in Emma's life at present, but little else.

"I used to gamble with him from time to time," Sir Archibald said. "You know he's put Miss Liston on the table more than once. Sometimes her hand, sometimes her virginity. He's just never lost. But some day he will, Abernathe. Someday *someone* will win her from him. Then she'll be no one's prize. Is *that* what you want in a duchess?"

There was a cruel tilt to Sir Archibald's mouth and James threw his drink aside. He caught the man's lapels with both hands and shook him.

"Get out of my house," he said, low and dangerous. "And never come back here again, you pompous prick. Or you shall be very sorry."

Sir Archibald squirmed and James shoved him away, sending him staggering across the lawn. It was only then he realized that the entire party had turned their attention to him, to *them*. Sir Archibald looked around at them, too, face red, and straightened his clothing.

"You'll find there are people not so worth defending, Abernathe," he sneered. "And enemies you'll regret making."

James took a step toward him, and Sir Archibald jerked away and hustled toward the house at the closest to a run he'd probably made since he was young.

"Ladies and gentlemen, why don't we all retire to the house to prepare for our picnic?" Margaret called out, but there was deep tension in her voice as she stared at James.

Guilt flashed through him. Meg spent so much of her time trying to mitigate any damage their mother might do to their reputations, and now James had just had a physical altercation with Sir Archibald, who was well known in Society. From the way people were staring and whispering already, it was clear *that* was going to cause a stir for some time to come.

Then his eyes caught Emma's in the crowd. She was watching him closely, her lips parted slightly. And suddenly he didn't give a damn about anything else. She had needed a champion against the bastard. He wasn't sorry he had taken on the role.

She deserved better than a life shackled to Sir Archibald, being seen as some pretty toy for his pleasure and none of her own. That wasn't the future he envisioned for Emma.

The crowd began to move toward the house and Meg walked to him, her gaze still even on his. He forced himself to focus on her, letting Emma fade into his peripheral vision as her mother came to her and they walked up to the house with the others.

"What in the world was that, James?" Meg asked under her breath.

He shook his head. "I'm sorry, Meg. I shouldn't have made a scene and embarrassed you."

"What could you have against Sir Archibald that would make you grab him like that?" Meg pressed.

He always tried to be honest with his sister. He always had been, for in some ways it had always been them against the world. But right now he was reluctant to tell her the truth. "He was...*untoward* about one of our guests," he muttered.

Meg leaned in, eyes wide. "One of our guests? Who?" He was silent for too long and she grabbed his hand. "Did he say something about Emma?"

He pulled away. "Why would you guess that?"

Meg put her hands on her hips. "Because I know you. You don't give two damns about any woman at this party save one. Emma is the only woman I've ever seen you pay more than two minutes of attention to. Was it her?"

He nodded slowly. "Yes. Should I not have defended her?"

"Perhaps not so strenuously," Meg said, and she was watching him even more closely now. "What is between you?"

"Who?" he asked, his voice rough.

"You and Emma, you great lout," Meg said with a laugh. "God, it must be something if you are trying so hard to pretend it away. I mean, you asked for her to be seated next to you, you danced with her last night, I catch you watching her all the time and you threw an acquaintance out of our party on her behalf...so what is it?"

He hesitated. Partly because he knew Meg wouldn't approve of his ruse with Emma. Partly because it was much more complicated than just that. He knew it. He didn't want to admit it out loud.

"Are you interesting in...courting her?" Meg asked slowly. When he didn't answer immediately, his sister clapped her hands together. "Oh, Jamie! That is wonderful! I have long worried about this drive of yours to have your revenge against Father by destroying your own future. A life alone punishes you more than him. And I adore Emma, I truly do. I'm so glad you will pick someone who is bearable and not some brainless chit."

She looked so happy that James could hardly breathe. Hardly speak. And yet he must, for he wasn't about to let Meg float through the rest of the party with this joy in her heart only to have it crushed. That was something their father would have done. Their father would have taken great pleasure in making Meg feel like a fool.

James wanted nothing to do with that.

"Meg," he said, but she was still talking about Emma. He cleared his throat. "Margaret!"

She stopped and stared at him. Her smile fell. "What is it?"

"I'm not...courting her," he said softly. "I'm only going to...pretend to court her."

Meg's brow wrinkled. "What?"

He drew in a short breath. God, but this was difficult. He could already see the beginnings of disappointment on her face. Disappointment in him.

"She needs help garnering fresh attention," he said. "You must have noticed how much more she's been getting with just a little from me."

"Pompous, James," Meg said.

"True, *Margaret*." He shrugged. "And I...I recognize you don't approve of my desire to avoid marriage, but it exists. At that first ball back in London, I was besieged. I don't want it, any of it. So if I pay some extra attention to Emma, it also helps me."

Meg shook her head, just shook it back and forth for what seemed like an eternity. Then she whispered, "Does she know that your attentions are untrue?"

"Of course!" he burst out, lunging to catch her hands. "Please tell me you do not think me so cruel as to do this without her knowledge, to purposefully play her for a fool. Please tell me that you don't think me even worse than Father, Meg."

She stared at him a moment and then her expression softened. "Of course not. You could not be so cruel, it is not in you. I suppose I am just...shocked that Emma would go along with something so dishonest."

James straightened and released her hands. Once again, his hackles were raised in defense of Emma. "She was reluctant," he said. "But you cannot truly judge her harshly. After all, her life is very different from yours."

Meg's face twisted just a little. "Yes, my fate, my future was sealed long ago."

He wrinkled his brow at the tone of her voice, but tried to remain focused on his defense of Emma. "Yes. You have never had to worry about your future. I made sure of it. Emma has none of those protections. And she's suffered for them. She would be a fool not to give herself a chance at marrying...well."

He said the last more slowly, for he found it difficult to form the words somehow. And when he pictured Emma in a marriage, his stomach actually turned.

Which he ignored as Meg let out a long sigh. "I suppose you are right."

"I am," he said softly. "If you must be angry with someone about this, please let it be me. Emma is a worthy friend and I would never want to ruin your relationship."

She bent her head. "You haven't, James. I am simply...disappointed. I thought you really were beginning to like Emma. I hoped..." She trailed off. "Well, I suppose it doesn't matter what I hoped now. I know you will not be turned from a path once you have decided to take it. But I do not approve."

"That is duly noted," he said.

Meg turned and looked up to the house. "I should go up and make sure all the arrangements have been properly made for the picnic."

James nodded, but as she stepped away he called out, "Meg?"

She peered back over her shoulder. "Yes?"

"You won't...interfere in our plan will you?"

"No," she said with clear reluctance. "I won't stop you."

He relaxed a little at her vow. He knew she would not break it. That wasn't Meg's personality. She kept to her promises and always had.

"Thank you."

"I'll see you shortly," she whispered, and walked away.

And though she had agreed to keep his secret, although she had acquiesced and promised not to change her attitude toward Emma, he still felt as though he had done something very wrong.

Something he wondered if he could fix.

CHAPTER ELEVEN

Emma stepped out of her chamber to find her mother already in the hallway waiting. And waiting rather impatiently, if her tapping foot was any indication.

"Good afternoon, Mama," Emma said with as bright a smile as she could manage in the face of her mother's focused expression. "Are you looking forward to the picnic?"

Mrs. Liston's eyes lit up in mercenary glee. "Not as much as you should be, Emma, for I have heard a rumor."

Emma slowly counted to five in her head before she said, "A rumor, Mama?"

Her mother caught her hands and leaned in. "The Duke of Abernathe's very public and rather physical argument with Sir Archibald, the one that led to Archibald storming away on his horse…it was over *you*."

Emma's lips parted in disbelief as she stared at her mother. There had been much buzz amongst the guests on the walk back to the house earlier in the day as to what could have caused such a shocking and public confrontation between the men. Emma had been curious, of course, for she had never expected James to act in such a way.

But over her?

"No," she said slowly. "That cannot be possible."

Her mother was almost bouncing now. "Oh, but they say it is. He didn't like the attention Sir Archibald was paying to you earlier, and here we are."

The blood in Emma's ears was rushing and her arms had begun to tingle, but she fought to keep a serene face as her mother prattled on and on. Was it possible this was correct, that James had almost fought with another man over *her*? That was taking their ruse mightily far, for he had claimed to want to bring men to her side, not push them away. *Literally* push them.

"...an opportunity you cannot turn down, so you must put your best foot forward and catch Abernathe at all costs," her mother said, grabbing Emma's arm.

Emma shook her off as her words became clear. "Catch Abernathe?" she repeated.

"Yes. When we came here, I would have, quite honestly, settled for someone like Sir Archibald for you," Mrs. Liston said.

Emma clenched her jaw. "He is older than Father and he has a brood of awful, awful children, some of whom are older than I am!"

"And what other options did you have?" Mrs. Liston snapped. "But now I can see we must reach much, much higher. Emma, you could catch a duke. A *duke!*"

Emma could hardly breathe. Oh, this was exactly what she and James had planned together, but her mind still spun regardless.

"I will *not* catch Abernathe," she whispered.

Her mother arched a brow. "Not with that attitude. Emma, you must be aggressive now. And...oh, how shall I put this...you must fight dirty if the opportunity arises."

"Dirty?" Emma repeated, nervous now about her mother's tone.

"It is true, he might be reluctant, despite his actions today," Mrs. Liston said, rubbing her hands together. "But that cannot stop us. If you must then I would suggest you...you..."

"What?" Emma burst out.

"Compromise yourself with him," her mother finished.

Emma stared, her mouth agape with horror. "*Mama*, you

cannot mean that."

Her mother folded her arms, a smug expression on her face. "Why not? Sometimes that is the way these things are done. And you can bear it, Emma. You shut your eyes and you just imagine the wonderful life you could have and what you could provide for me. Picture the freedom from any damage your father could do, the freedom from fear of the unknown. It will make his touch bearable."

Emma shivered, for her mother was so in the dark. Not only did she have no idea of Emma's plan with James, she also didn't know that Emma had, for all intents and purposes, already compromised herself with James. Bearing his touch was not an issue. She couldn't stop thinking about it.

"Emma!"

Both women turned down the hall to see Meg coming toward them. She was smiling but there was something in her eyes, some tiny look that made Emma's heart skip a beat. Had she overheard this horrible conversation? Certainly Meg wouldn't want to be her friend if she knew what her mother had just said.

"Just think about it," Mrs. Liston hissed before Meg met them and linked her arm through Emma's.

The affectionate gesture soothed Emma a little as they made their way down the stairs toward where the others were gathered for their short walk to the picnic site, but she still felt an unease in her stomach. It seemed at all sides she was besieged with plots. And none of them felt right.

Emma slowly dropped back through the crowd of partygoers until she trailed behind them. Only then could she breathe again. The past quarter of an hour had been a nightmare, with James shooting her looks, her mother's suggestion ringing in her ears and Meg smiling and chatting with her, utterly oblivious to all the betrayals Emma was committing.

She felt like rolling into a ball and hiding away forever, but that wasn't possible. So the best she could do was provide some distance between herself and the others and try to regain some purchase on her emotions.

Something that became clear was impossible when she looked up to find James standing along the side of the path, leaning against a tree. She let out a sigh as she approached him.

"Waiting for me?" she asked.

"Hiding from *me*?" he retorted.

"No," she lied, for she had, of course, been doing exactly that. "I needed...I needed space."

He straightened up and looked at her more closely. "What's wrong?"

She worried her lip for a moment and shook her head. "Just...my mother is pushing me. And she told me..."

When she trailed off, he reached out and took her hand. She caught her breath as she looked up at him. His gaze was heated, hooded, and her body responded even though he was barely touching her. Everything felt hot and tingly and the world went blurry, the only thing in focus was him.

"What did she tell you?"

She drew in a deep breath. "That you fought with Sir Archibald over...over me." His face twitched, and in that moment she saw the truth. She would not have been more shocked if the man had started singing and dancing right there on the path. "You *did*?"

James nodded. "He said something very untoward. And I admonished him for it." His tone was dark and dangerous, and once again it hit her in the most inappropriate places.

"Something untoward about me?" she gasped. "He doesn't know about—"

"No!" James said. "Not about us. He just made some implications about his intentions toward you that I didn't care for."

She shivered, for she could well-imagine what Sir

Archibald had in mind. He had always spent a great deal of time staring at her chest, and whenever he touched her, it was like a snake curling around her skin. But still…

"You grabbed him, you pushed him, you sent him away," she stammered. "James, you…you made a scene."

"He deserved far worse than I did to him," he said. "But how did your mother know?"

She shrugged. "I have no clue. Someone overheard you, perhaps, or Archibald talked before he fled your house. What matters is that people are going to be talking about this. It is too good a story not to repeat."

"You seem troubled by this," he said, his brow wrinkling. "Why?"

"Aside from the fact you nearly came to blows over me? I am troubled because it casts too big a shadow on me."

"No, it puts focus on you, which was *exactly* our plan from the beginning," he said, but his tone was falsely bright.

She pulled away from him at last with more reluctance than she should have had and folded her arms. "If this is exactly what you intended when we began, then why do you sound tense, why is there concern in your eyes?"

His brow wrinkled and he stared at her. "I-I…I don't know what you're talking about," he said, and the negative emotions wiped from his face at last.

She shook her head. "You can't pretend it away, James. This obviously concerns you as much as it concerns me. While I appreciate this protectiveness you are displaying, I feel it is better that I just know the worst of it so I can be prepared."

"You see too much," he muttered as he ran a hand through his hair. "Emma, I'm not concerned about Archibald. He's an idiot and the gossip about his leaving will fade long before it does any permanent damage, especially if we choose not to address it so as not to feed it." He let out a short sigh. "There is…something else, though. And you're right, you should know about it."

Her heart began to throb as she stared at him, trying to read whatever was on his mind before he said it. Failing even as she came up with horrible scenario after horrible scenario.

"What is it?" she asked, barely above a breath.

"Margaret knows about our ruse," he said softly.

Emma staggered and he lunged forward to catch her arm, steadying her. She looked up at him, too close, too handsome, too perfect, and she could hardly recall how to breathe, let alone speak. He waited patiently, not trying to force her, not trying to fill the space between them with words.

"She knows we're pretending a courtship?" Emma asked.

He nodded once, and she let out a tiny, strangled cry. "*That* was why she looked at me so strangely. I thought it was my mother, what my mother said, but it was this. How does she know?"

He released her at last and motioned down the path. "We should walk so we aren't too far behind the others," he suggested.

She thought about fighting him a moment, but decided against it. He was correct, after all. Arriving together too far behind the others would open them up to impertinent remarks and even more encouragement about compromise from her mother.

They stepped forward together and Emma said, "Tell me, please."

He bent his head. "*I* told her, Emma."

She jerked her face toward his and found him looking at her. She swallowed hard, choking back the sense of betrayal his confession created in her chest. He couldn't betray her. They were nothing to each other, despite the kissing. She had to remember that.

"Why?" she whispered. "Why did you tell her?"

He was silent a long beat. "I have this huge group of very good friends," he said. "But the person who knows and loves me most is Meg. We are the only two who fully understand our...past. Our situation with our parents. I do not lie to her, not when I can help it. Nor does she hide things from me. She came to me, thrilled as could be about the idea that you and I were courting. I could not mislead her and let her be hurt in the end. So I admitted our ruse."

Emma wanted desperately to be angry at him for doing it, but she found she wasn't. Not when he explained himself in such a way. How often had she longed for someone to share things with like he described? She had no one as a confidante. In some ways, she was jealous rather than angry.

"I...understand," she whispered at last. "And I know it is for the best. I also wouldn't want to hurt Meg. I just wish..."

She trailed off, unwilling to confess her foolishness to this man. After all, he was not her confidante either.

"What do you wish?" he pressed.

She shook her head. "Nothing."

He stopped in the path and turned toward her. "We will crest this hill in fourteen steps, Emma. When we do, the picnic site will be just on the other side. Everyone will be watching for us, waiting for us, and this conversation will be over. There is no time for pretending. I have done something that I do not regret, but I also have no illusions that my confession doesn't affect you. So if you wish something, tell me what it is now."

His tone was sharp and dark, his gaze focused and compelling. In that instant, her wishes morphed from ones regarding Meg to ones about his mouth. His lips on hers.

She blinked those thoughts away. "I wish that I could have stayed friends with Meg. I did truly like her."

He stared at her. "Why wouldn't you stay friends with Meg?"

"Why would she want to be after this?" she asked, humiliated by tears that stung her eyes. "What she must think of me!"

"Meg likes you, she understands why this path is one you felt you must take. If anything she is angry at me for—"

He cut himself off and jerked his gaze away. She leaned forward. "What is she angry at you for?"

"It doesn't matter," he said, and looked back at her. "I had one other topic I wanted to address with you before we join the others. At least broach it for further discussion."

Her lips parted. He had neatly cut her off from anything deeper in his heart and even though what they shared was not real, she felt disappointed. She cleared her throat. "What is that?"

"Your father, Emma," he said softly.

All her thoughts of Meg, of her mother's inappropriate suggestions, of wanting to kiss James, they all vanished in an instant and the world felt like it slowed to half-time.

"My…father," she repeated, the words feeling like they were yanked from her body with painful force.

He nodded. "Yes. I've heard things here and there. I wanted to bring up the subject because of our situation."

"Our situation," she repeated. "How does my father have anything to do with our *situation*? You aren't truly courting me. You have no fear of what he could—" She broke off and caught a ragged breath. "What he could do. I do not wish to discuss him."

He stared at her in true surprise. "I am not trying to pry, I just want to help."

"You can't help," she said. "And you *are* prying."

"Emma," he said more sharply. "It is a perfectly reasonable question."

"Yes, for a man who would be my husband," she snapped. "You have made it clear you don't want that role in reality. So you have no right to ask me about private things. After all, would you wish to tell me about your mother? About why she…why she is the way she is?"

He recoiled, turning his face like she had physically struck him. His jaw flexed as he kept his attention focused away from her. Finally, he said, "I see what you mean. Come then, let us return to the others."

He motioned her toward the hill and began to walk again, without waiting for her. She stared after him a few steps before she scurried to catch up with him. He was quiet the entire way over the hill and then he smiled and all the pain, all the upset was gone. No one would ever guess they had quarreled from the way he waved to the group and gave some explanation about a rock in her slipper.

But even though no one else knew the truth, she did. She knew she had very likely ruined everything between them. And even though most of that everything was predicated on a ruse, her chest still hurt at the idea that this man now thought differently of her.

And there was nothing she could do to change that.

James sat at his desk, staring with unseeing eyes at the estate paperwork strewn across the top. He'd been in here for an hour, trying very hard to concentrate and failing miserably. All he could think about was Emma.

The picnic had been successful as far as Meg was concerned, but for James it had been torture. First, his attention to Emma didn't seem to be working entirely as he'd hoped. He still caught the interested glances and whispers from some of the woman at the gathering. Certainly many of the freshest debutantes put their eyes elsewhere, but there were other women who gave him looks. The Countess of Montague, a notorious flirt, kept putting herself in his way, batting her eyelashes and talking about…honestly, he didn't know what exactly.

Of course, that didn't trouble him as much as the fact that *Emma* had sat as far from him as possible, never looking at him. Worst of all, *she* had become the focus of several of the men in attendance. Unlike at the ball, these had been men of higher quality. Younger, many with money, there was even one viscount in the group.

In that respect, his plan was working as far as Emma was concerned, but he did not celebrate that fact.

There was a light knock on the door and his body clenched. He knew who it was. He knew what he had to do.

"Come in," he said as he rose to his feet.

The door opened and Emma stepped inside. He caught his breath. She was dressed for supper, in a sunny yellow gown with a hand-stitched skirt. The color brought out the highlights of her hair and made her a bright beacon in what had been a dark evening so far.

"You wished to see me," she said, her tone formal and uncertain. She didn't look at him.

"Come in. Shut the door."

She looked at him then with uncertainty and whispered, "That isn't appropriate, James."

"Neither is the conversation we must have," he said on a sigh. "Please, Emma. Close the door."

She took in a long breath, almost as if she were steadying herself, and did as she had been asked. She didn't move toward him, though, but stayed at the entryway, hand ready to open the door again.

"If you want me to leave, I understand," she said softly. "But it will take some convincing to get my mother to do so."

He stared at her, seeing now the way her hands trembled, how pale her skin was, and worst of all, the redness of her eyes that indicated she had been crying.

He stepped toward her almost without willing himself to do so. "Emma, I didn't call you here to ask you to leave. Why would you think I would want that?"

She swallowed and her voice was thick as she said, "Our conversation earlier today wasn't exactly positive. You are doing me a favor with your bargain and I rewarded you with dismissal and rudeness. Why would you wish to keep me here? You don't need me."

In that moment, he wanted nothing more than to cross the distance between them and fold her into his arms. To hold her against his chest in comfort and whisper that he *did* need her. Even though he didn't want to. Even though he fought it with every fiber in his being. He was coming to need her.

He didn't. Instead, he cleared his throat. "I asked you to tell me something today about your father. And you made a good point that I have not told you anything personal of myself. Since you know my mother and you have seen her at her...at her worst, perhaps you *are* owed that explanation."

"What?" she breathed, bright eyes going wide with surprise. Now she left the safety of the door and moved in his direction a few steps.

"You asked me why my mother is the way she is," he said, each word stabbing him in the heart. "The answer is simple. She married a man she did not love and one who most definitely did not care for her."

She swallowed. "She was unhappy?"

He nodded slowly. "I have never known her not to be unhappy. She drinks to forget it, I suppose. And *that* is why I do need you, Emma. I have no interest in entering into the same kind of arrangement."

"A marriage, you mean," she whispered. "What you saw between your mother and father is why you do not wish to marry."

"In part, yes."

"But couldn't you—" she began, and cut herself off. Like the topic was too intimate. It was, but he found he wanted her to speak freely.

He moved toward her a step. "Couldn't I what?"

"Couldn't you find someone you *did* love?" she whispered. "Someone who loved you?"

He lifted his chin and shook his head. "That is a fairytale talking, Emma. Those who find true love are very rare. Even with those who do, it doesn't always last. No, I know my limits and I don't expect anyone else to save me from them."

She stared at him, and in that moment he saw something in her eyes that terrified him. He saw pity. Like she knew the truth of him and felt sorry for him.

And then she moved toward him again, only this time she didn't stop until she reached him. Slowly she lifted her hands, touching his cheeks. He didn't pull away, but gazed down into her eyes. He wanted to run from her, but an equally strong part of him wanted to stay. She was looking into him, deep into his soul, and there was some tiny sliver of him that *wanted* her to see the truth. Like he wanted her to do exactly what he claimed he didn't desire.

Save him.

"*That* is where the sadness comes from," she whispered.

As what she said sank in, his eyes widened rapidly and shock spread through him. He'd spent a lifetime teaching himself to hide his emotions. As a boy he'd done it to protect himself. As a man, the driving reason was little different. But what was clear in this moment was that Emma saw him. She *saw* what he didn't want to admit to himself that he felt, let alone say it or show it to anyone else.

Terror gripped him as he jerked his face from her hands. "There is no sadness, Miss Liston, I assure you," he said, his tone clipped and as unemotional as he could make it.

She let him pull away, but didn't retreat from him. She stood her ground like she belonged on it. "There is sadness in everyone, Your Grace," she insisted. "No one gets through this world without some of it."

"Well, there is none in me, Emma," he ground out, frustration in his tone at her insistence that he face himself. Face her. He clenched his teeth and fought her the only way he knew how. "Certainly, there is none right now. Right now I am standing in a private room with a beautiful woman and the last thing I am thinking of is my troubles. What I am thinking about is this."

He dropped his mouth to hers and kissed her. A punishing kiss, a hard kiss, but she didn't pull away from it. On the contrary, she opened to him right away, inviting him in, taking what he offered with only a soft sigh of acquiescence.

His fear and his sadness, his anger and his frustration, they melted into her, and he gentled his lips on hers as he tugged her even closer. Her arms came around his back and she moved her head so he could deepen the kiss. Lose himself in it and in her.

And he did. He forgot every other thing in the world except her taste, her feel. He drowned in her and he didn't care if he ever came up for air again.

He pushed her backward, turning her until she leaned into the edge of his desk. He wanted to feel her against him, he wanted to touch her, he wanted to make her come like he had before. More than that, he wanted to bury his body deep in hers and shatter with her.

But that wasn't possible.

He pulled away from the kiss and stared at her. Her gaze was bleary and unfocused, her lips red and full from his kisses, her breath coming short and raspy.

"I want to touch you again, Emma. I want to do more than just touch you, even though I will keep my vow not to claim you."

She bit her lower lip gently. "Yes," she whispered in answer to the question he hadn't asked. "Please."

The please nearly unraveled him right then and there, but he managed to gain some control over his lust. He smiled at her, lifting her more securely onto the edge of his desk. Then he began to slide her skirts up as he sank into a chair, and positioned himself as he parted her legs.

She stared down at him, eyes wide, body trembling. "What are you doing?" she whispered.

He glanced back up at her, wicked because wicked was the one thing he could control. "Tasting you, Emma. I'm going to taste you."

CHAPTER TWELVE

"Taste me?" Emma gasped, her hips arching of their own accord as James pressed each warm hand on one of her bare thighs and parted them a little wider.

"Oh yes," he purred, opening her drawers so he was looking right at her sex.

Heat flooded her cheeks at his intense perusal. "I really don't understand what you mean by—"

Before she could finish the statement, he leaned in and pressed his mouth to her, tracing his tongue along her folds.

Intense sensation mobbed her and she jolted against him, which only drove his tongue harder against her and made what he was doing all the more powerful. He held her steady and licked her again, this time spreading her folds open for better access.

She knew she should protest. That she should crush this wanton creature he awoke in her and tell him no. He would stop. She had no doubt he would.

But she *didn't* stop him. Instead, she collapsed back a little on his desk, opening herself wider to him as he stoked and stroked with his tongue. He found the little nub of nerves just at the top of her sex and circled it languidly, making her shudder as electric pleasure sizzled through her. But then he backed away and went back to making love to her body with his wicked, talented tongue.

She arched against him, unable to stop the tide of sensation that was washing through her, over her, threatening to drown her with its intensity. He looked up at her and their eyes met as he pleasured her.

"I would love nothing more than to do this for hours," he panted between licks. "But I can't. Not now. So…"

He trailed off and she let out a tiny cry as he focused his mouth on her clitoris. He sucked her, gently at first, then harder, and she clung to the desk edge with one hand while she covered her mouth with the other to hold in the cries of pleasure she could no longer control.

The sensations were building, higher, faster, stronger than the last time he'd touched her and then, almost without warning, the bubble of release burst. She jolted her hips against him as wave after wave of intense pleasure rocked through her. She was drowning, she was flying, she was lost and she was saved all at once, and he never relented as he licked her harder and harder and harder.

Finally, after what seemed like a blissful eternity, the tremors subsided and he lifted his head from between her thighs to smile at her. Heat burned her cheeks at the intimacy of what they had just done, but she returned the expression nonetheless.

He caught her hand and helped her sit up then get to her feet. She straightened her skirts, aware for the first time of the harsh, hard bulge in his trousers. She knew very little about sex, but her mother had told her the barest necessities. This was proof that he wanted her.

She glanced up at him and found him watching her. He shrugged one shoulder. "I'll find satisfaction on my own later."

She swallowed hard. He meant he would…touch it, she supposed. The very idea was intriguing, and her heart began to race, tingles flooding her and settling to the very place he'd been licking mere moments before.

Great God, but she was a wanton.

She turned away from him and continued to fix herself. He cleared his throat. "Now, wasn't that a better use of our time than engaging in some pointless conversation?"

She froze and slowly pivoted to look at him once again. There was a smirk on his face. It was an expression she knew far too well from over the years. A look people got when they'd pulled one over on her. Or played some kind of joke.

She stared at him, hands beginning to tremble. "Did you...*do* what you just did because you wanted me or because you wanted to put me off?"

He shifted—it was barely perceptible, but she saw it. "Of course I wanted you," he said.

She shook her head, keeping her stare trained on him when she wanted nothing more than to turn away. Walk away. Run away.

"You lie," she whispered. "You didn't like my questions or my observations. You wanted to stop me so you used my weakness against me. You found a way to distract me that you knew I couldn't resist. Oh, it was a far kinder way than some others have done in the past, but you were still hiding from me."

"And what if I was?" he asked, his tone growing cooler as he folded his arms across his broad chest. He was no longer her gentle lover—he was Society's golden child again, and she was just a wallflower. "It isn't as if *you* revealed any secrets to me when I asked for them."

She faltered, for he wasn't wrong. He'd asked about her father and she'd refused to respond. She'd dug deeper into his past, into his motivations about never marrying, and he had done the same, albeit with far more pleasant results.

"It seems we are both cowards," she said at last, bowing her head as she backed toward his office door. "Too afraid to give anything for fear it will open us to hurt, to betrayal. We will protect ourselves to a bitter end. And it will be bitter, James. Because we both know that the path we are on will guarantee we end up alone. Even if I find a husband here, even if you one day accept that you must find a wife...we will still be alone."

He stared at her, gape-mouthed, and she turned away as she clutched at the door handle. Her hands were shaking so hard she could hardly turn it to free herself from this room, this space, from this man, from the things she, herself, had said, that felt so real and so painful.

"Your Grace," she whispered, and fled from him.

She entered the hallway, her breath coming hard and fast, and stumbled blindly away from him and what they'd just done. Not just physically, but how they had built a wall between them. She'd never expected anything less, but seeing it and feeling it there now stung her in ways she'd never imagined. All she wanted was to go upstairs, lie down and be alone. Away from others, away from James, away from the truth about herself that her accusations about him had revealed.

"Emma?"

She froze at the sound of Meg's voice floating down the hallway behind her. She drew a deep breath, fighting desperately to keep herself from showing her turmoil on her face, and spun to look at her friend.

"Meg," she said with false brightness. "I didn't see you."

Meg smiled, but there was hesitation in the expression that made Emma's heart sink. Of course there would be. James had already told her his sister knew of their ruse. Now Meg would confront her about it and there was a strong possibility that Emma would lose a friend.

Her heart hurt with the thought.

"I think we need to talk," Meg said, slipping up to her and motioning to a parlor door just up the hallway. "And this is the first chance we have to be alone, so will you join me?"

Emma hesitated. That urge to run away was even stronger now. And yet there was nothing to it. She couldn't run, not really. This kind of disappointment always caught her when she tried. It was better to just let it happen now and be done with it.

"Of course," Emma managed to say past dry lips.

She followed her friend into the parlor and watched as Meg shut the door behind her. She leaned against the barrier and stared at Emma.

"My brother told me something today," Meg said.

Emma bowed her head. Part of her appreciated how direct Meg was. There was no pretending with her. No dancing around uncomfortable topics. And yet she wished they could pretend just a little while longer, because somehow Meg had become important to her in the brief time they'd known each other.

"Yes, I know," Emma said. "He told you about our arrangement. He mentioned your conversation to me on the way to the picnic. And he told me about your disappointment."

Meg stepped forward. "I *am* disappointed, Emma. Truly."

Emma shivered. Right now her game with James seemed worse than ever and she longed to escape it. But she had earned this censure and she would have to just face it.

"I understand," she choked out. "And if you do not want to be my friend—"

Meg caught her breath and reached out, grabbing Emma's hand. Emma clung to her, like Meg was a life raft on a boiling sea.

"Of course I want to be your friend," Meg said. "Gracious, my relationship with you was never predicated on your relationship to James. You are my friend regardless of what happens between you or what agreements you two make outside of our friendship."

Emma nearly buckled with emotion at those words. Tears leapt to her eyes, but for once in this awful day they were tears of relief. She wouldn't lose Meg in all of this.

"I'm so glad," Emma whispered.

Meg smiled as she drew Emma to the settee and they sat together there. "My disappointment stems from the fact that I think my brother would have an easier time of it if he had the support of a woman like you. I *wanted* your courtship to be real."

Emma stared at her, shocked firstly that Meg would want her brother tied to a woman with so little in the way of prospects, with no influence and with questionable family connections. But also shocked that what Meg said revealed something of her own heart.

Because in that moment Emma realized some part of her

also wished that this courtship were real. That what had just happened between her and James in his office was the beginning of something greater, not just a way for him to hide from her.

"Do you mind if I ask you a question?" Emma asked.

"Of course."

"Why *is* your brother so opposed to marriage?" She knew some of that answer, of course. He'd told her about the terrible consequences of the loveless marriage of his own mother, but she knew there was more.

And she was willing to go behind his back to discover what that more was.

Meg let out a long, pained sigh. "Father was so cruel to him."

Emma drew back in surprise. She'd never known the previous Duke of Abernathe, for he had died long before she came out in Society, long before she was being taught or grilled about those who were her betters. But she'd never assumed he'd been cruel.

"How?" she whispered. "Why?"

Meg shifted in discomfort. "James wouldn't want me to speak about this. He would consider it a betrayal, I know. His past is private—only his closest friends know even a glimpse of it."

Emma nodded slowly, disappointed that she would be kept from the truth, even if she understood Meg's reasons to keep her in the dark.

"Do you care for him?"

Emma gulped in a breath at the unexpected question and the focused way Meg was staring at her. "I-I—you know it is a ruse."

Her friend was watching her and her expression was serious. "Yes, I do. But sometimes when I've seen you together, I've sensed something deeper than what could be construed as a ruse. I wonder if you care for James. If there is *any* part of you that wishes there could be more between you than just some elaborate game he has concocted in order to protect himself...to protect you?"

Emma stared at her hands, clenched tightly in her lap. Meg was dancing too close to the truth, too close to the edge. Emma didn't want to reveal so much of her heart, and yet she found herself unable to do anything but just that.

"I do care for him," she whispered. Saying the words out loud stole her breath and she struggled before she continued. "Even though I know there is no hope for a future with him. There is something about him that makes me want…more."

Meg smiled, and there was no mistaking her triumph. "I knew it."

"But Meg, there is no indication whatsoever that he feels anything for me," Emma said swiftly. "Nor that he has a desire to change any of his plans for me. You must know that it is a losing battle. The best I can do is follow what he wants, try to use his attention to find another match."

Meg wrinkled her brow, and there was understanding on her face. Something that went deeper than a mere empathy for Emma. "Yes, I know that sometimes we can't have what we truly want," she said softly. "Though I would wish more for you and for my brother than an arrangement you didn't want and a lonely, empty existence."

"I appreciate your thought, but…I must accept what is," Emma said. "I know that."

Meg bent her head and took a long breath. "James was not the firstborn son," she said without looking at Emma. "Our father was married before our mother."

"He was?"

"Yes. His first wife died giving him his heir. And then the boy died years later, as well, in an accident."

Emma caught her breath. "That poor man."

Meg shrugged. "I do not know how he was with that first family. It's hard to imagine he was ever kind or loving, for I certainly never saw that capacity in him. But whether he truly cared for his first family or not, our father was a duke and continuing his line was his obsession. He needed an heir, so before his mourning period was even over, he courted and married our mother. They produced James in short order. I was an attempt at a spare, and a disappointment to him, for certain."

Emma reached for her, catching her hand. "I'm sure not, Meg. No one could do anything but like you."

Meg's smile was sad. "Thank you, Emma, but I promise you my father did not. He used to tell me so to my face before he stopped talking to me entirely when I was fourteen."

"He stopped talking to you?" Emma repeated, her jaw dropping at the very idea of such cruelty.

Tears leapt to Meg's eyes but she blinked them back. "He said I was my mother's problem. But it wasn't just me. He didn't *like* any of us. He despised us for being the replacements for the family he truly desired. In truth, I appreciate being ignored. James wasn't and he bore the brunt of our father's hatred. One of my earliest memories is the duke slapping James across the face so hard across the face that he split his lip."

"How old was he?" Emma whispered.

"Eight? Perhaps nine?" Meg swallowed hard. "As my brother bled and cried, Abernathe berated him for not being Leonard, our half-brother. The true heir, as our father always called him. He *loathed* James and that broke my brother's heart."

Emma covered her mouth with her hands and held back a sob of pain at the story she was being told. She could hardly imagine how much that must have hurt James.

"He hated my brother for being who he was. And James grew to hate him in return. He does not want to be like our father," Meg continued.

Emma nodded. "I can see why he wouldn't after what you say he endured."

Meg let out a long, heavy sigh. "Our father only wanted him to carry on his legacy. And so James's desire is to end that legacy once and for all. Not marrying is a punishment for the previous Abernathe, one exacted after his death. Or perhaps it is a penance, for our father, for James himself." Meg shivered and at last a tear slid down her cheek. "So now you know the truth."

Emma put an arm around her friend and stroked her hair as Meg rested her head on Emma's shoulder. "I'm so sorry you both went through such an ordeal," she said softly.

Meg nodded and let out a sigh. But as she comforted her friend, Emma found herself thinking of James. What Meg had told her made everything she knew about him, everything she saw that he didn't want her to see, make perfect sense. And she felt for him. She cared for him.

Even though both those things were incredibly dangerous to her own well-being, she still felt them, and she still wished that there was something she could do to ease his pain.

CHAPTER THIRTEEN

Avoiding Emma didn't help. James fisted a hand against his desk top and glared at it as if it had done something to offend him. And in truth, he *was* angry at himself. After their prior encounter twenty-four hours ago, James had tried to stay away from Emma, hoping it would reduce this strange sensation in his chest. But it hadn't.

Sitting far from her at supper the night before had only made him wonder what she was saying to the gentleman she *was* seated beside. Later, when games were played, he had only watched, hating that he wanted to congratulate Emma when she won or give her advice when she was losing a hand of whist.

And when he had been asked about her—coyly, by Lady Montague, who had sidled up to him with her batting eyelashes and inviting smiles—saying glowing things about Emma was just too easy.

"Idiot," he muttered to himself as he flexed his fist open and stretched his stiff fingers.

"What have you done now?" Graham asked as he entered James's office and shut the door behind himself.

James shook his head. This felt like such a private topic. Too private, even for his best friend. But when he looked up at Graham, he knew he would discuss it. Graham had always been able to milk the truth from him. He never rested until he had. It was why he was more like a brother to James than just a friend.

"I have no idea what I've done," James muttered. "Something entirely foolish, it seems."

Graham's teasing expression slipped to something more serious and he took a spot across from James and leaned forward, draping his elbows over his knees. "What's this about? You've been out of sorts for days."

James tilted his head back and stared up at the elaborately carved ceiling. He let out a long breath, but couldn't find the words to explain what he wasn't certain he entirely understood himself.

"Is this about that woman? Emma Liston?" Graham asked.

James stared at him, taken aback by Graham's gentle tone. His expression was no different. Graham already seemed to know the answer to the question he'd asked. James gritted his teeth. "Yes," he admitted softly.

Of course Graham seemed unsurprised by that answer. "I see. I thought you had that all worked out, that your ruse was perfectly planned. What's wrong?"

James pushed to his feet and walked away. "You needn't gloat, you know. I hear it in your tone."

"Why would I gloat?" Graham asked. "Unless I was right and you've fallen in love with the girl."

James pivoted to face him, feeling all the color drain from his face. "In love with her? No, of course not. Of course not. Of course I don't love her."

"Of course," Graham repeated. "You say 'of course' three or four times and it makes your lack of feeling toward her infinitely clear. So you are *not* in love with her, of course not. Then what is it? Her pushy mother? The strain of lying to everyone? She trods on your feet when you dance together? What is it?"

James looked down to find his foot tapping wildly and he forced himself to stop before he ground out, "She can…*see* me."

Graham wrinkled his brow. "See you?"

Now that it had been said, James wished he could take it back. Oh, Graham knew his history, as did Simon. But they never spoke of it. He *never* let it affect what he did or what he took or how he behaved. Now he was about to lay something bare and he wasn't pleased about it.

"She sees what is real," he clarified. "Not just what I choose to show."

"Such as?" Graham pressed after a pause that felt like it stretched for an eternity.

"She said she saw sadness in me," James whispered, trying not to react to that claim once again and failing, just as when she'd said it and it had felt like she'd slipped her soft hand around his heart and squeezed.

Graham's lips parted. "I see."

"It is...entirely disconcerting." His voice sounded choked and his throat was tight.

"Of course it would be, to be exposed in such a way by a woman who you've really only begun to know in the past few weeks."

James nodded, but in truth he didn't feel like that. Sometimes it felt as though he'd known Emma a lifetime.

"I don't want her to see," he said, more to himself than to Graham.

Graham let out a sigh. "But what she says is true, isn't it?"

James shut his eyes, not wanting to look at his best friend. "Of course not," he lied. "I'm the life of every party, you know that better than most."

"Oh yes," Graham said. "You dance and you laugh, you take risks and you seduce the ladies. You are, on the surface, every joyful and carefree thing in the world. But I know you."

"Yes, you do," James admitted, looking at him at last. "Most people only see me at my best, but you and Simon have seen me at my worst."

"We have. I saw you after your father's fit when your marks weren't perfect."

James flinched. "He hit me so hard, I thought he'd knocked my teeth out."

"I wanted to kill him," Graham said, his face growing red

with just the memory.

"You would have, if Simon hadn't held you back," James said with a shake of his head and the shadow of a smile.

"And I saw a great many other days when the previous Duke of Abernathe treated you like a dog and not his son. I saw you when your father died," Graham continued.

"You and Simon were there for it all. It's why I arranged the union with Meg," James said. "I wanted one of you to be my brother in truth."

A shadow crossed Graham's face briefly, but he pushed it aside. "I will always be your brother," he said softly. "No matter what happens."

"And I appreciate that," James said, sliding a hand through his hair. "But it's different with Emma. As you said, I've only known her for less than a month. Having her be so perceptive is...I don't know."

"Well, maybe that is worth something, James," Graham pressed. "Maybe the discomfort is a sign that it is time to be real. To allow someone else to see past the exterior. Maybe this is an opportunity."

"What are you suggesting?" James asked. "That I make this courtship real, that I consider marrying her, despite all the vows I've made to the contrary?"

Graham shrugged. "I always thought your drive to avoid wedlock punished you more than it could ever punish a dead man."

James considered the comment a moment. Meg had said something similar and he'd dismissed it, but now it was harder. He could truly picture what they each suggested. There was a flash of fantasy through his mind. Of a life that would be possible with Emma. One with pleasure and laughter...but also vulnerability. The more she knew him, the more she would see. It wouldn't just be hints of sadness then. She would know his anger, his pain, his fear...

He frowned. "No, I don't think so," he said.

Graham pressed his lips together in concern. "Well, then

you only have two more options. You can abandon your plan completely…"

James shook his head. "No, that would hurt her. I don't want to hurt her."

Graham arched a brow, as if that statement proved something on its own. Then he continued, "Your other option is to make tonight a big show. Play out the ruse, give her so much attention that it is clear she is desirable. Once that's done, let her go to pursue whatever options come out of it."

James nodded. He knew Graham was right but the knowledge felt…hollow somehow. He pictured Emma finding someone else to love, to marry, to share all her passion that was just under the surface and he felt…empty.

But then, he'd always *been* empty in truth, no matter how he pretended otherwise.

"I'll think about it," he said.

Before Graham could answer, there was a light knock on his door. He turned to face it and said, "Enter."

The door opened and Emma stood on the other side. She looked at him and his heart actually stuttered. She was dressed for the upcoming ball, and the blue color of the gown she wore brought her eyes to life.

"Emma," he breathed.

She turned her head and seemed to notice Graham for the first time. She actually jumped. "Oh, I'm sorry. I didn't realize you were here, Your Grace."

Graham sent James a look filled with meaning. "I was actually just leaving, Miss Liston. A pleasure to see you again."

He executed a small bow and then slipped past her and left them alone. She entered the room at last and slid the door shut behind her.

He flashed to the previous day when they'd been alone in this room. To tasting her, to bringing her pleasure. God, how he wanted to do it again.

But she cleared her throat and said, "James, do you want me to leave?"

Emma watched James's expression change at her question. When she entered the room, it had been an open one, a heated one. Now a guard came down over him and his voice was hard as he said, "You've only just arrived, Emma. Why would I wish for you to leave?"

She shook her head. "Not leave this room. Leave your home. Leave the party. Go back to London with my mother."

His eyes went wide. "This is the second time you've suggested you leave here. Why are you bringing it up again?"

There was a hint of desperation in his tone now that she understood. It made her want to move forward, into his arms. It made her want to touch his face and soothe him. She didn't.

"James, we agreed to a ruse, but this…this is getting out of hand, isn't it?"

He folded his arms. "How so?"

She almost threw up her hands in frustration at his reaction. "Well, you aren't exactly pleased with me, are you?"

He moved forward and she stopped breathing. "Not with you, Emma. With myself."

She blinked at that unexpected response and stared up into his face. His emotions were so tangled there she couldn't determine one or another above them all.

"Why?" she whispered.

"Damn it," he burst out, and turned away from her. He walked to the fire and stared into it. She wanted to say something, to push, but she didn't. She forced herself to remain still and steady, waiting for him.

Finally, he turned. He stared at her. He looked her up and down and made her feel stripped bare. Naked emotionally as well as physically. Then he made a soft sound in the back of his throat and he was moving on her.

He caught her arms, drew her against him and lowered his

mouth to hers. She lifted into him, melting into his heated kiss, surrendering to the power of it and of him. This wasn't what she'd come here for, but she couldn't resist it. As dangerous as that admission was, now that the bottle had been uncorked, she could no longer fit her feelings back inside.

He drew back at last and looked down at her, panting. "You were *not* supposed to be irresistible, Emma. I don't want you to be."

She shivered as he pulled away from her. He kept his back to her and she had no idea what to do or say.

An answer she did not have to find when the door to the study flew open and her mother burst into the room. Emma's heart sank at the bright and hopeful expression on her face. One that fell when she saw James far across the room and Emma where she stood.

"Oh, excuse me, Your Grace," Mrs. Liston said, sending a side glance to Emma. "I heard my daughter was seen entering this room, but I had no idea you were with her."

James had turned upon her entry and was now staring at her. Emma's heart sank, for his expression was bland and bored, the same one she'd seen him give to a dozen grasping mamas over the years. Now she was no better than those women who he disregarded with such ease.

"Good evening, madam," he said.

"Do I need to call a vicar?" her mother said with a chuckle.

Emma lunged forward. "Mama!" she gasped, cheeks burning. She couldn't bring herself to look at James again. "That is *enough*."

"Oh, hush, child, I'm only teasing," Mrs. Liston said, her gaze still on James. "Though this *is* inappropriate, Your Grace. You alone with my daughter with the door shut."

He was quiet a moment, long enough that even her mother shifted under his accusatory silence. He cast a swift glance at Emma, and she prayed he could see she had not arranged this ridiculous display.

"Of course you are correct, Mrs. Liston," he said softly.

"My behavior is untoward. I apologize to you and to Miss Liston."

"Oh no," Mrs. Liston burst out. "Of course my daughter is so very honored by the attention you pay to her."

"Mama!" Emma hissed, grasping her arm.

Mrs. Liston shook her off. "We will leave you now, Your Grace. But I certainly hope we shall have the honor of you dancing with Emma tonight."

James inclined his head without verbally responding, and Mrs. Liston caught Emma's hand and drew her to the door. She went with her mother, incapable of doing anything else in the face of this new humiliation. But as they exited, she cast one final look back at James.

He was staring at her, face still impassive, and it was in that moment she realized that he'd never told her he didn't want her to leave. And after this display, she could imagine he would want nothing but exactly that.

CHAPTER FOURTEEN

Emma stood against the wall, her head bent and her lips pinched. James felt his stomach turn as he watched her, for her pain was clear. All he could think about were the three options Graham had offered him hours ago. He could send her away, he could make one last attempt to help her or he could simply claim her as his own and be done with this madness.

But the last was impossible. It felt impossible. He'd vowed never to marry as a punishment to his father, and that was part of the reason he resisted his duty. But there were other reasons, too. Chief amongst them is that Emma's ability to see into his soul was abjectly terrifying to him. Letting *anyone* so close was an exercise in pain.

He'd learned that from his father, if nothing else. How many times had the man drawn him in, especially when he was small? He'd pretend to change, pretend to care, only to cruelly cast him out just as swiftly. James had learned that love wasn't permanent. It never could be.

He could not allow Emma any closer than she already was, but that didn't mean he didn't still want to help her. He'd seen what she was up against during the intrusion of her mother earlier in the evening. Mrs. Liston was so desperate that she might ruin everything for Emma if they didn't act swiftly.

So he drew a harsh breath, steeled himself against whatever foolish feelings were trying to break through within him, and crossed the ballroom toward Emma.

She seemed to sense his approach, for when he was about halfway across the floor, she looked up and found him. Her eyes went wide as she straightened up and her lips parted.

He was lost. He wanted to take her mouth, he wanted to take her body, he wanted to hold her up against him and let everything warm and wonderful about her fill him in his empty spaces.

But he couldn't allow that. He stopped before her and held out a hand. "Dance?" he asked, incapable of making the question more formal.

She stared at his outstretched fingers for far longer than any other lady in his acquaintance would have done. Then she nodded speechlessly. He took her hand, jolted once again by awareness at the action, and led her to the dancefloor where they began to move together.

She was silent a long time. He allowed it for he had no idea what to say to her, how to face her when she was far more than he'd ever expected her to be weeks ago when his plan was hatched.

Now that seemed like a lifetime ago.

Finally, she cleared her throat and whispered, "You told me that your father was why your mother behaves as she does. It is the same with me and mine. His issues are…well known. I'm certain you must be aware of them."

He stared at her, shocked that she would at last address his earlier question to her. After everything that had happened since, he hadn't thought she would bring down that particular wall.

Yet she did. She trusted him and that made his chest swell with pride. That she would offer this glimpse into herself meant something. He wanted it more than he cared to admit.

"I have heard a few whisperings about Harold Liston, I admit."

Her face drained of color at those words, and for a moment she stumbled in her steps. He steadied her, keeping her upright as he examined her face.

"*That* is what my mother fears most," she said in a tone that was barely audible. "That eventually those whisperings will becoming shouts and any chance I have at the future she wants for me will be dashed at last."

"The future she wants?"

She nodded. "A good marriage, one that will offer not just me a place in the world, but her."

His jaw tightened. How he understood about being forced to take care of those around him, even to his own detriment. "That is a great deal to lay on your shoulders."

She shrugged one of those shoulders and said, "It is what has been expected of me for as long as I can recall. The weight can be…heavy, especially since I have failed in obtaining what she wants for so long. But it isn't as if I have any choice in the matter. Going to live in the countryside as a spinster is not something I am allowed to think about."

He wrinkled his brow at the unexpected option she put forth. "Is that what you would want, to live a life alone? Never marry, never become a mother yourself?"

She tilted her head. "You are one to talk. You have a duty and you will not fulfill it, either. You are willing to go so far as to pretend to court a woman in order to avoid forming a real connection with anyone."

He looked deep into her eyes. "I think we have a real connection."

Her lips parted slightly and her eyes glazed with a hint of desire. She shook it away. "But not permanent, Your Grace. So we are both led by the shadows of our fathers. You because you do not want to be like him, me because I fear the consequences of his actions."

He pulled back slightly at her statement. How did she know about his father? He had barely spoken to her on the subject.

Unless Meg had revealed him.

"What are your father's actions?" he asked, drawing her away from the subject of his pain.

She sighed. "He gambles, he engages in scandalous affairs,

he brawls. He does whatever he likes."

"That sounds like how you once described me," he said. "Golden? Untouchable?"

He expected her to laugh at his gentle teasing, but instead her jaw set. "On his best day, my father isn't half the man you are, James. And he has never been golden. Everything he does has a cost. He just doesn't always pay it."

"You do," James said gently.

She nodded, and her upset was clear. "*That* is why my mother considers him such a danger, even though she forgets all that the moment he comes home and gives her a crumb of attention."

He shook his head. "She would turn her back on all he's done?"

"As you said, that is what love does," she whispered, her voice cracking and her gaze suddenly intense.

He shook off the effect of that pinning look with difficulty. "Makes her forget that she believes him to be a danger? *Is* he one?"

He thought of what Sir Archibald had said about Liston's gambling with Emma's future. At the time he had believed it was just nasty baiting, but now…now he feared it might be true, Especially when Emma hesitated far too long for him not to know the answer even before she spoke again.

"I don't know," she admitted. "To himself at the very least."

The music began to fade and James found himself frustrated by that fact. He had been taken aback by her ability to see him, truly see him, but tonight he had finally gotten a glimpse into her.

He stepped away to perform a bow as she curtsied, then he lifted her hand to his lips and placed a kiss across her gloved knuckles. He felt her tense, saw her pupils dilate with the same desire that coursed through his own veins. The one he had not expected, but had come to crave as much as water or food.

"Thank you, Emma, for trusting me. And I want to help you. I'll do everything in my power to do so."

She pulled her hand from his, her face turned as if she didn't like that answer. "Thank you, Your Grace," she murmured before she turned and left him.

He watched her weave through the crowd on what appeared to be unsteady legs, and wished he could go after her. But he didn't. Because to save her, truly save her, would be losing himself.

Emma stood on the terrace, clutching the rock wall and staring out into the dark night. The cool air did nothing to calm her, for her mind kept running back her dance with James.

She had been trying to pretend she could play this game with him without losing. But she wasn't sophisticated like him. She wasn't able to guard her heart the way he had clearly taught himself to over the years.

So when she looked up into his dark eyes, she realized how much she cared for him, craved him. Not just his intoxicating touch, but *him*. She wanted his heart, she wanted his soul, she wanted to belong to him, not just for a night or for the duration of a party, but forever.

"Idiot," she cursed at herself, clenching harder at the wall.

"You want him."

She started, turning to find her mother standing at her shoulder with a smug smirk on her face. "What?" Emma burst out, too loudly. "Who?"

"Abernathe," her mother said, drawing out the name slowly. "You want him, don't you?"

Emma shook her head. She didn't trust her mother enough to make her a confidante. "Don't be silly, Mama."

"It isn't silly," her mother said, reaching out to cover her hand. All it succeeded in doing was pressing her palm into the cold, rough wall. "You could have him, Emma, and in the process save us both. You know what to do."

Emma turned her face. "I will *not* compromise myself and betray him by forcing him into a union he does not desire."

"Betray him?" her mother repeated, her expression shocked. "My dear, you must not be so naïve. He may pretend to be something heroic in here, but a man like that would just as soon cut your throat as save you, no matter what he pretends right now. You are at war and you must do anything to win."

Emma yanked away from her. "Listen to me, Mama. I will *not* compromise myself and force his hand. Stop asking me to do so."

Her mother huffed out a breath. "Then you doom us both."

With that she hustled back into the house. Emma was ready to follow when she caught a flutter of movement from the dark edge of the terrace. She turned toward it, heart pounding, and watched as James stepped out of the shadows. The heart that had been pounding now sank as she watched him come toward her, his face twisted with emotion, his gaze focused entirely too hard on hers.

"How much did you hear?"

"Enough," he said softly. He said nothing else, but bent his head and kissed her. While his other kisses had possessed her, claimed her, this one was gentle. Soothing, and she sank into it because she needed his strength and his support in that moment.

When he pulled away, she let out a shuddering sigh. "Thank you."

He smiled. "We *will* work this out, Emma."

She stared up at him, his handsome face lined with worry. She was falling in love with him. She knew that. Perhaps she'd always *been* a little in love with him. It explained why his mere presence made her nervous. But that had been an unrequited feeling, a silly notion she'd never fully believed was possible. Men like him didn't want women like her. She'd accepted that.

But now the world was turned over on its head. James Rylon, Duke of Abernathe, *did* want her. He proved that every time he touched her. It was too easy to be lulled into the possibility that friendship and desire could turn to love when they wouldn't. Not for him.

He would never allow that.

She pressed her shoulders back and stepped away from him. "My mother is wrong about a good many things, James. But in one thing, she is correct. This *is* a war. Not with you, not in the way she believes. But a war it still is. And I must stop waiting for something to happen, waiting to be saved. In the end, I must fight it for myself. Otherwise I will end up a causality. And I might very well drag you down with me."

He stared at her. "What are you saying?"

"It's time for me to fight my own battles," she whispered, wishing her words sounded as brave as she wanted them to. Wishing her heart felt brave, too. "You have positioned me on the battlefield, after all. It is time for me to act. Good—good night, James."

She held his gaze for a long moment and then turned away. He whispered her name. It floated to her on the wind and she nearly turned back. Nearly rushed back into his arms where she most certainly did not belong.

But somehow she found the strength not to. She kept walking, went inside and surveyed the crowd. She observed each eligible man in attendance, analyzing them, and at last she found her mark. With a smile that did not reflect the loss she felt in her soul, she strode across the room to Meg.

Her friend smiled as she reached her. "Enjoying the night air?"

Emma tried not to think of her stolen moments on the terrace with James. The moment when she'd realized she had to let him go. "It was a bit cold outside, actually. Meg, can you do me a favor?"

Meg nodded. "Anything in the world, Emma. You know that."

Emma squeezed her hand, grateful for the kindness of this woman who she had grown to adore in the few weeks they had been friends. "Yes, I do know. Will you introduce me to Mr. Middleton?"

Meg blinked a few times and both women looked across the room to the gentleman in question. He was older than Emma by at least fifteen years, but his age did not hang on him like an ill-fitting vest as it did with many men. He was of a similar rank to her own father, though he had taken his connections and parlayed them into minor financial success and respectability. He had also lost his wife three years before and had two children.

In short, he was not reaching too high like she had been with Abernathe, nor too low.

And when Emma looked at him, she felt nothing.

"Emma," Meg breathed. "What about my brother?"

Emma caught herself before she let out a pained gasp. She refused to meet Meg's eyes as she said, "Abernathe has helped me a great deal, but I know I must take these next steps myself. I can't wait around for someone else to save me."

"That isn't what I meant," Meg whispered.

Emma turned toward her friend. "I know it isn't. But James…he cannot give me what I need. I'm not even sure he would want to. And no matter what I think or feel, I cannot be so foolish as to pretend I have all the time or choices in the world."

Meg bent her head. "You are trapped."

"Yes." Emma nodded. "And I must make the best of it."

Meg laughed, but the sound was pained rather than pleasurable. "Well, no one understands that concept better than I."

Emma tilted her head, really seeing the pain on Meg's face for the first time. Really seeing that trapped expression that she knew so well, herself. "Meg, do you not want-"

Meg shook her head. "Let's not talk about what I want. It doesn't matter. Come, let us meet your Mr. Middleton."

They crossed the room together and Meg made the introductions as a good hostess. And as a good friend, she then found a reason to leave the two alone. Emma moved through the motions of a short discussion with the man, but was hardly attending even as they chatted and he asked her to dance.

She followed him to floor, and as they began to turn together, she saw James reenter the ballroom. His gaze found her, locking on her and her partner. His jaw tightened and his fists clenched at his sides. But he didn't move on her.

And she turned her face and concentrated on the future, not the past. And not a fantasy she could never really have.

CHAPTER FIFTEEN

James stalked through the garden, not paying attention to anything around him. He didn't give a damn about flowers or morning dew or chirping birds. Right now he was alive with frustration and an anger he couldn't fully process. All he knew was that he had been kept awake all night by both. And every time he did find sleep?

He dreamed of Emma. Emma in his arms. Emma opening to him. Taking Emma.

Alternating between blind rage and a cockstand was not a pleasant way to fill the hours.

He careened around a corner and came to a stop. Standing there, staring up at the house, was Simon. "Crestwood?"

Simon started, turning toward him with a flush to his cheeks that almost looked guilty. "James, didn't see you there. You're up early."

"I couldn't sleep," James admitted. "Looks as though you couldn't, either."

Simon shrugged. "It's a regular affliction for me lately, it seems. Walk with me?"

James stepped in beside his friend. "What troubles you?"

"Nothing that can be fixed," Simon said, his tone very soft but also hard as steel. "What about you?"

"I'm sure you and Northfield have already discussed my problems at length," James muttered.

Simon hesitated and then nodded. "Yes, if nothing else we are able to talk about you. He mentioned you're struggling with...with this ruse you've decided to play out with Emma Liston."

A ruse. James almost laughed. It seemed from the very beginning it had been more than a mere ruse.

"I don't like feeling this way," he admitted softly.

"Which way?" Simon asked.

"Like I'm having something taken from me. It isn't even something I want."

Simon came to a halt in the pathway and folded his arms. There was a snap to his expression, a hard line to his mouth, and he glared at James. "You aren't having something *taken* from you. Trust me, I know that feeling and this is not it. You are *surrendering* something. You fear it, so you'll just let it go. Throw it away like it means nothing when it's obvious it means everything."

James stared. Normally Graham was the one who provided blunt words and hard advice, while Simon softened everything to make it more palatable. But in that moment, Simon almost looked like he wanted to hit James.

"It wasn't supposed to be—"

"Oh, fuck supposed to be, James. Damn it!" Simon spun away, running a hand through his hair. "You've spent your life trying to live up to and run away from your father's legacy. And now you're willing to lose something..." He looked back at the house. "Lose something worthwhile just to make a point to a dead man. Well, if that's what you want to do, you don't deserve to have it."

James drew back farther. "Simon..."

"Forget it," his friend grunted. "Just forget I said anything. Grimble was looking for you earlier. I'll...I'm sorry."

Without another word, Simon turned and stomped off, not toward the house, but the stables. James watched him go, both troubled by his words and confused by the passion with which they had been spoken.

He finally walked to the house, Simon's voice still ringing in his head. His friend was, for all intents and purposes, calling him a coward.

Worse, he felt like Simon might be right.

He entered the house and Grimble rushed to greet him. The butler's face was pale and he looked apologetic. James steeled himself for whatever trouble had been caused by whichever houseguest.

"I hear you've been looking for me, Grimble," he said, forcing his tone to be even as he shrugged from his heavier outer coat and handed it off to the servant.

"Yes, sir. I'm sorry to disturb you with this, sir. I had no idea what else to do."

James wrinkled his brow. Grimble was normally cool as anything, but his stammering words and sweaty brow put James on high alert.

"I'm certain whatever it is that has happened, we can work it out. Tell me what's amiss," he said, making his tone calmer to reassure the man.

Grimble clenched his hands together in front of him. "We have an arrival, Your Grace. And he was insistent he must join the party. It took everything in me to convince him he must wait for your approval. But he's *very* loud, sir, and increasingly demanding, and I—"

James held up a hand to stay Grimble. "Who?" he asked. "You said an arrival, but we are certainly not expecting anyone else at the party. So, who is it who has intruded?"

"Mr. Harold Liston, sir," Grimble ground out.

James straightened at the name. His lips parted in surprise. "Miss Emma Liston's father?" he breathed.

Grimble nodded once. "Yes."

"Do Mrs. Liston or Miss Liston know that he has arrived?" he asked, thinking of Emma's quiet confession on the dancefloor, of her palpable fear when she talked of this very man not twelve hours before.

Grimble swallowed hard before he said, "It is still very early and I did not think they'd yet be up, sir. Though Mr. Liston was demanding he and his trunks simply be taken to his wife's chamber."

James ran a hand through his hair. "It would give the woman an apoplexy. But they must be told. Have someone go up and fetch them. I assume Mr. Liston has been put in a parlor?"

"Yes, sir," Grimble answered.

"Good, then he isn't roaming the house. So have the Liston women brought there as soon as they are able. The servant sent does not have to say that Mr. Liston is here. Have the person who escorts them knock twice and I will join them in the hall and tell them this news myself."

Grimble didn't seem at all surprised by this strange directive. He simply nodded. "I shall, sir. What else can I do?"

"Just tell me where Liston is," he said.

"The blue room."

James strode off from him without another word, down the long, twisting hall until he reached the blue room. Even before he got there, he heard the intruder inside, moving around and talking very loudly to himself.

James set his shoulders back and pushed open the door. As he did so, a man turned from the fireplace and looked at him. James could see the resemblance right away. Emma had inherited those eyes from her father, though Liston's were not as alive nor as kind as his daughter's.

"The Duke of Abernathe," Liston said, the slight slur to his words telling James that the man was drunk despite the early hour.

Of course, James wasn't one to judge. His own mother was likely still in her stupor, as well. But then, she hadn't intruded upon a private party, nor was she threatening anyone at present, unlike James's unwanted houseguest.

"You should fire that butler of yours," Liston continued. "Rude bastard. He wouldn't allow me up to see my own wife."

James lifted his chin. "You have no quarrel with my butler. Grimble has done exactly as I would wish him to do. As you were not on the guest list for our party, he was not about to give you access to the home or our guests until I had approved it."

Liston straightened up and glared at him. "So I must gain your approval, then, boy?"

James's nostrils flared and he moved forward a long step. "Do not forget yourself, sir, nor the disparity of our rank. I am the Duke of Abernathe and I shall be treated as such, or you shall be removed in a matter that you won't find comfortable."

Liston seemed to consider that statement and inclined his head. "Certainly, Your Grace. I apologize for my rudeness. I have just been made to wait for over half an hour and I would only like to see my family."

James clenched his hands at his sides. Liston was doing what he could to make himself look good. James knew better what the truth of him was.

"Mrs. Liston and your daughter will join us shortly," he said softly. "But as they are guests in my home, I am responsible for them. I must ascertain what your intentions are in coming here."

Liston's eyes narrowed. "*He* said you were circling. Not that you could have any true intentions."

"He?"

"Sir Archibald," Liston said with a cool smile.

James took a step closer as his body went cold. Archibald, whom he had sent away not a week before for his nastiness toward Emma. The idea that that viper had run straight to Liston was troubling, indeed, considering what he'd said about their shared gambling habit.

"What do you want here?" James said.

Liston's smile faltered a little and he folded his arms. "I want to see my wife and my daughter, Your Grace. You see, I have news for them. News they will both wish to hear. And it is not news I have any intention of giving to you. So why don't you simply get them here?"

Emma looked at her reflection in the mirror as Sally made the last few adjustments on her hairstyle. The maid had been chattering all morning as she did her duties, but Emma had hardly attended. Her thoughts kept going back to James.

As they always seemed to do now.

"But last night was so successful for you, Miss Emma."

Emma blinked as her attention was brought back to her servant. She frowned. "I assume that means Mama's maid is telling you whatever my mother said?"

Sally shrugged. "Claudia and I share a room in the servant quarters and she has never been reserved."

"It is why she and my mother get along so well," Emma muttered. "Yes, I suppose last night's ball went well. I danced regularly."

Sally's smile was bright. "That must be a relief. You will have some options for a future."

Emma stared at her reflection again. A relief? No, she didn't exactly feel relief. Nor happiness in her current circumstances. She *should*, but that didn't make it so.

There was a knock on the door, and she sighed as she rose and nodded to Sally to answer. It was her mother on the other side, and she looked far too excited for Emma's taste.

"Good morning, Mama," Emma said, moving toward the entryway. "I didn't expect to see you up so soon."

Mrs. Liston grinned. "I would not have been, except that you and I have been summoned by Abernathe."

Emma caught her breath as she stared at her mother. Slowly, she turned and nodded at Sally. "That—that will be all," she managed to choke out.

Sally looked disappointed that she wouldn't get to listen in, but bobbed out a curtsey and slipped from the room.

"You look miserable," her mother snapped when they were alone. "Didn't you hear me? I said the Duke of Abernathe has asked for our presence. Together!"

Emma could hardly hear over the rush of blood in her veins, but she tried to keep herself calm. "Did he say what he wished to discuss with us?"

"No," her mother conceded, "but there could only be one thing."

"And what is that?" Emma whispered.

Her mother slapped her arm. "He wishes to ask for your hand, Emma. It could be nothing else."

Emma had a moment where her entire body filled with joy. That joy revealed a truth she had been trying to fight for so long. She wasn't falling in love with the man—she *did* love him already. Worse, she wanted a future with him.

But that didn't mean she thought her mother was correct in her assessment of the situation. James had made it abundantly clear he had no intention of offering for her. And she had been trying to accept that and position herself for some other future.

"I would not bank everything on that," Emma said. "There could be many topics Jam—Abernathe would want to discuss with us."

Her mother smiled in triumph at her near-slip of using James's given name so freely. "I don't think so. Come, we must not keep him waiting a moment longer."

She clasped Emma's arm and all but dragged her down the hall and the stairs to the main level of the house. At the bottom of those stairs, a servant awaited them.

"His Grace is waiting for you in the blue room," the young man said. "Please follow me."

He turned and guided them through the long halls. As they followed, Mrs. Liston gripped Emma's arm tighter. "You see. Such formality!" she said in a stage whisper that could likely be heard four rooms away. "It can be nothing less than a proposal."

Emma's cheeks flared with heat. "Please don't make a scene, Mama," she whispered. "We know nothing. Let us not act like fools."

The servant stopped at a closed door, shot them a look over his shoulder and then rapped twice. To Emma's surprise, he didn't then enter, but waited in the hallway for the few seconds it took for James to answer.

James glanced into the hall, nodded to his servant and stepped out to join them. He shut the door behind himself and waved the footman off.

Once he was gone, James smiled at first Emma, then her bouncing mother. Emma's chest tightened and her throat closed. He looked very upset. Something was wrong.

"Good morning, ladies," he said. "Thank you for joining me."

"We wouldn't have missed it," Mrs. Liston said, grinning at him. Emma fought to hold back a sigh. Her mother clearly had no observational skills in the moment. She was so wrapped up in this proposal she believed was forthcoming, she couldn't read James's frown, the darkness in his stare, the increasingly gentle tone he used, like he was leading someone to their grave.

"What is it?" Emma whispered, holding his stare.

For a moment, his gaze faltered and darted away, but then he brought it back to her and held firm. She saw his hand stir at his side like he wanted to touch her, and in that wild moment she wished he could. She wanted to cling to him, to steady herself with this strength.

But she couldn't.

"There is no easy way to say this," he said. "So I will simply state it. You have a visitor who has come to this house to see you. A man I fear neither of you may wish to see."

Emma felt herself swaying. "Who?"

"Mr. Harold Liston," James whispered. "Emma, your father is here."

CHAPTER SIXTEEN

Emma stared at James. He was talking, but it was like she was being held under water as she watched his lips move. He sounded incredibly far away and hollow as her mind spun on what he had just said.

Her father was here. *Here*! He had come all the way from London to the shire of Abernathe, found Falcon's Landing and stormed this castle like an invading army.

He had come *searching* for her and her mother, rather than simply waiting for their return to London in another week's time. And *that* could not be a piece of good news.

"—why you would believe this would not be a happy bit of news, Your Grace," her mother was saying, her tone falsely bright. "I didn't expect my husband to join us here, but of course we will *both* be most pleased to see him."

Emma took in her mother's words with a slow shake of her head. Even in this moment, when it was obvious James knew of their troubles with her father, her mother was more concerned with appearances than protection. Worse, Emma knew that the moment her mother laid eyes on her husband she would turn to a tittering debutante, swept away by a handsome man.

Because she always did.

"Is he…in there?" Emma asked, flicking her hand toward the room where James had exited from a moment before.

He nodded slowly. "Yes."

"Then in we go," her mother said, and all but pushed past James to open the door.

James looked at Emma as Mrs. Liston did so. Then he reached out and traced just his fingers across her own. "I'm here," he whispered. "I'm *here*."

She shivered at the intimacy of both his touch and his words, but then she stepped away. James said he was here for her, but that was not permanent. If she leaned too heavily on him, when he was gone she might not recall how to bear her own weight.

"Thank you," she murmured, and then moved past him into the parlor where her father now stood with her mother. He was holding Mrs. Liston's hand and she was staring up at him with adoration, despite all her statements about how dangerous and unreliable he was. It had always been that way with them.

Emma watched her father as he was distracted by the bride he found so easy to discard. It had been nearly a year since she'd last laid eyes upon him. She was always surprised by how young he still looked. His hair maintained its thickness and luster despite the growing gray at his temples, and his eyes were bright. Of course, not having to bear any responsibility would do that to a man.

"There's my Emma," he said, dropping her mother's hand as he moved across the room to her. He leaned in to buss her cheek and she bore it as best she could.

"Father," she said softly.

"Papa," he corrected. "No need for such formality. Not when I come with such news for you."

Emma's heart jumped to double time. "Such news" didn't sound like a good thing. Her father's plans and schemes never worked out, and she and her mother would be left gathering up the pieces in the end.

As always.

"What news?" Emma managed to squeak out.

Her father patted her cheek, then looked past her to James. He glared at the duke and Emma's stomach turned. Leave it to her father to force himself into someone else's home, then dare to be offended that he wasn't welcomed.

"I'm famished and I have not exactly been met with politeness in this house. I assume you have quite the spread for your guests, eh, Abernathe?"

"Quite," James said back, his tone clipped and dangerous.

Her father didn't seem to care, for he clapped his hands together. "Most excellent. Then let us eat before I tell you the good news. Come, my love."

He caught her mother's arm and guided her from the room. Emma could hear her tittering as they left, and shut her eyes with a long sigh.

"Emma," James whispered.

She spun around. "Perhaps you are correct in your low assessment of love, James. Look at what a fool it makes my mother."

"I want to help," he said.

She shrugged. "So you keep saying, but in this case there is nothing you can do. He is here now and…and likely all is lost. I should have been more focused. I should have tried harder. I shouldn't have gotten caught up in—" She cut herself off and shook her head, not daring to look at James now. "It doesn't matter."

She said nothing else and left the room. James let her do so, following behind her without a word, just his presence.

And it comforted her even though she knew he could do nothing for her now.

They entered the breakfast room, which was buzzing with talk and laughter from the guests as they perused the offerings on the sideboard and sat together chatting and drinking tea or coffee.

But as Mrs. Liston entered with her arm locked through her husband's, the conversation stopped and all eyes turned to the couple. Emma could hardly breathe as she watched her mother beam with what looked like genuine happiness and coo, "And look who has joined our happy party—my husband, Mr. Liston."

"Quite a crowd, Abernathe," Mr. Liston said with a laugh as he entered the room and drew his wife to the sideboard. Emma caught him looking at the women in attendance, saw him sizing them up.

She shook her head. Some things never changed.

James moved past her into the breakfast room and she felt him subtly draw his hand across her back as he did so. The warmth of his fingers as they brushed her spine made her sink momentarily into his comfort.

But then he was gone, talking to those in the room, obviously trying to divert some attention from the return of her wayward and publicly troubled father. She appreciated the effort, though it clearly did no good. As she entered the room, she felt the eyes on her. She heard the little whispers.

Though she wasn't hungry, she joined her parents at the sideboard and dished herself a small plate, then moved to the table. Meg was sitting at one end and motioned to her, so Emma followed the directive and sat beside her friend. Beneath the table, Meg threaded her fingers into Emma's and squeezed gently. Yet another place of support to be found in this family.

One she would lose if her father destroyed her at last.

Mr. Liston set both his plate and her mother's down and flopped into a chair just a few places down from Emma's. He began talking—too loudly, as always—and her heart sank.

"Chin up," Meg whispered. "It's always best to pretend you don't even notice the humiliation."

Emma shot her a look, thinking of that night at the ball when the Duchess of Abernathe had been so very drunk. Of course Meg understood what she was going through. Slowly she straightened in her chair and smiled at her friend.

She was going to get through this with her dignity intact, even if her social standing at last collapsed completely at her feet. Dignity had value.

"And what brought you as such a late addition to our party, Mr. Liston?" the duchess was asking as she heavily sugared a cup of coffee and drank it with a heavy sigh.

He grinned and his gaze flashed toward Emma. "I have news for Emma. Good news, in fact. And what better time to share it?"

James speared him with a glare. "Perhaps your news would better be given to your daughter in private, Liston."

The crowd bounced their attention from Emma's father to James in a heartbeat, then back to Mr. Liston as they awaited the response to the duke's quiet admonishment.

"We're amongst friends," Liston said. "Aren't we, Emma?"

Emma swallowed hard. Her father wanted to share whatever news he had right now because it was going upset her. That was the only reason he could possibly have for wanting to do this in a public forum. In this room, with all these people watching, she would not be able to show her upset in order to maintain a semblance of decorum. Nor would she be able to refuse him whatever he had arranged for her.

"Of course we are," Mrs. Liston said, still staring at him in adoration, though her voice trembled a fraction and she shot Emma a concerned look.

"You are to marry, Emma," Mr. Liston said with a wide grin when she didn't answer his question. "I have arranged for you to wed Sir Archibald."

Once again Emma felt as though her head had been dunked under water. Blood rushed to her ears and she swayed in her seat as the room erupted in surprised sounds. Meg held her hand tighter, Emma could feel each of her friend's fingers against her skin, but she didn't move. She didn't speak. She didn't breathe.

She just stared at her father and saw the flicker of guilt in his eyes. Something had happened that had forced his doing this. Something where he had traded her hand to save his own skin.

"Archibald was a guest here, I believe. Took quite a notion to you and came straight to me to make the arrangements. He'll be rejoining the party shortly. I'm sure you don't mind, Abernathe." When Emma still could find no words, her father shook his head. "Well, come then, girl, say something," Mr. Liston said with a chuckle. "I've arranged a good match for you,

you *must* have something to say."

"She is silent because Emma has been keeping secret her own news, Mr. Liston," James said as he slowly rose to his feet. Emma watched him, well aware of his tall, strong body as he unfolded it. As he positioned himself toward her father, it was a subtle threat of his superior position and strength.

"J-James," she whispered, not even caring that she was addressing him inappropriately in front of people who would gleefully talk about it. They had enough fodder now, what was a little more?

"News?" Mr. Liston repeated, giving Emma a concerned glance. "What news does my daughter have?"

James locked eyes with her, and in a split second, Emma saw what he would do. Meg must have sensed it too, for she sucked in a long gulp of air before he spoke again.

"Though Emma may appreciate the work you have done on her behalf to match her," James said. "I'm afraid it is impossible. You see, Emma has already agreed to marry *me*."

She pushed to her feet. "James," she repeated.

"Yesterday," he continued softly as he looked at her evenly. "I intended to officially ask her mother for her hand this morning when you made your arrival."

At that, the room erupted in complete chaos and Emma felt blackness filling her vision. In the distance, she heard James shout out, "Catch her!"

And then the room went very dark.

CHAPTER SEVENTEEN

James carried Emma's limp frame into a parlor and laid her out on the settee. A trail of people followed him, keeping him from privacy as he knelt beside her and looked into her pale face with concern. There was his mother, Meg, Mr. and Mrs. Liston and of course four of the five members of the 1797 Club in attendance. Only Simon did not join them, for he had not returned from his ride to be present for the announcement of the "engagement".

James glanced up and met Baldwin's eyes. "Thank you, Sheffield," he said softly. "She might have struck her head if you didn't move so quickly to catch her."

Sheffield arched a brow. "I could not risk injury to the future wife of one of my best friends, could I?"

He heard the question in Sheffield's tone. He saw it on the faces of Brighthollow, Roseford and Graham, as well. But there would be time to open a discussion on that subject soon enough.

Right now, he had to focus on Emma.

"Emma," he said, smoothing his hand along her cheek. "Emma?"

Her eyes fluttered and slowly opened. For a moment, she only stared up into his face and he saw just the hint of a smile on her lips. A smile just for him, and his heart throbbed at it. But then her gaze shifted to the rest of the room, to the crowd of people staring at her, and the smile faded as she struggled to sit up.

"Oh no," she moaned.

He placed a gentle hand on her shoulder. "You fainted, Emma, so lay still. Just rest a moment before you pop up and repeat the action all over again. I might not catch you so easily as the Duke of Sheffield did."

He was teasing, but she didn't register any pleasure at it. She just kept staring around the room at those in attendance.

"James," she whispered.

He nodded. "It's all right."

"This is all very dramatic," his mother said with a sniff.

"Hush, Mother," Meg snapped, her concern for Emma clear. "Emma had every right to lose her senses after that awful scene in the breakfast room."

James held Emma's gaze for a moment, hating the pain he saw there, the humiliation, but worst of all...the resignation. She was resigned to a heartbreaking fate, despite his attempt to save her with his announcement. But he was not going to allow that now any more than he had been willing to allow it a moment before. He was going to fight for this woman.

Somehow she had managed to inspire that in him.

"Everyone out," he said, his tone firm. "Everyone but Mr. and Mrs. Liston."

He lifted his gaze and met that of each of his friends. And, of course, they understood him. Quietly, they began to hustle his mother and the servants who had trailed in to help to the door. In the end, only Meg stayed of those who had been ordered to leave.

She moved forward and edged James out of the way to kneel beside Emma on the settee. Emma's eyes filled with tears. "I'm sorry," she whispered. "I'm so sorry I've spoiled everything."

Meg's lips parted and she grasped Emma's hand with both of hers. "You've spoiled *nothing*. So there is no need to be sorry. Ever."

She leaned in to kiss Emma's cheek, then turned and did the

same for James. He read her pointed stare as she did so. The one that begged him to follow through on what he'd claimed in the breakfast room, the one that told him, without words, that he should marry Emma. And marry her quickly.

And perhaps not just for her own good.

He nodded slightly and Meg pushed to her feet. She whispered, "Where is Simon? He wasn't with the others."

"Crestwood took a ride," he said, thinking briefly to his friend's troubled behavior in the garden just before James's entire life had been blown to pieces. "He needed to clear his head."

"Clear his head?" Meg repeated, her gaze lighting with concern. Then she nodded once. "I'll find him and explain what's happened. I know you'll want him to know and to be here with us. With you."

James smiled at her before she left, closing the door behind herself and leaving him alone at last with Emma and her parents. Emma sat up, waving him off as she slowly got to her feet. When she seemed steady, he spun on Mr. and Mrs. Liston.

"Out with it," he snarled, barely keeping himself in check. "What did you do, Liston?"

"James," Emma whispered, and he turned toward her to find her staring at him, eyes wide and filled with fear.

"I'm not going to let him hurt you," he declared, holding her gaze so that she would see he was utterly serious. She swallowed, her face filled with disbelief that he would champion her, which of course made him want to do it all the more.

He retook his position facing Harold Liston and glared at him. "Talk."

"He didn't *do* anything," Mrs. Liston said, gripping her husband's arm tightly. James shook his head, disgusted that this woman would take her wayward husband's side over her daughter's. "Tell him, Harold. Tell him that you only made a good arrangement for Emma, not realizing she had another suitor in the wings."

Liston's gaze darted away. "Sir Archibald approached me

in the past few days, that's all. He just wanted to discuss Emma with me."

It was obvious he was lying. His gaze couldn't focus, his cheeks filled with color, he was sweating and he drew his arm away from his wife and paced the room restlessly.

James was about to press harder, but Emma stepped forward. Her hands were shaking, but she didn't look like she would faint again. No, in that moment she looked angry. Righteously angry and utterly beautiful in it.

"What did you do, Father?" she demanded. "Stop lying to James. Stop trying to look like the hero for Mama and tell me the truth. Look at me and tell me what exactly you did!"

"He gambled with you," came a voice from the door. They all turned and found that Sir Archibald himself was now standing in the parlor entryway. He smiled at the group at large and continued, "And it wasn't the first time. Just the first time he lost."

Emma felt an urge to scream. Just sit down on the floor, clench her fists and scream out her rage and pain until it emptied out of her chest and allowed her to take a full breath again. But as she stared from Sir Archibald and his smug smile and back to her father and his sheepish look, she didn't do that.

Instead she folded her arms and took a long step toward Mr. Liston. She held his gaze—she refused to let him look away—and then she said, "For once in your life, tell me the truth."

"It isn't *my* fault this happened," her father responded, throwing up his hands as he whined. "He wanted to play cards, what was I to do?"

"Say no," James said softly as he stepped up beside her and gently placed a hand on the small of her back.

She looked up at him, thinking of what he'd said in the breakfast room. What he'd claimed he'd asked her, how he'd claimed she'd responded. But he couldn't really intend to follow through on wedding her. That was madness.

"He's *never* been able to say no," Archibald laughed. "So we played until he'd lost his blunt, and then his horse, and then I suggested a new wager. Emma's hand."

Mrs. Liston covered her mouth with both hands, her breath coming hard and harsh now. Emma could see that her mother wanted Emma to come to her, to comfort *her*, but Emma didn't. She couldn't. She'd spent a lifetime doing so, a lifetime wiping her mother's tears as she swallowed her own. In this moment, she had no strength for it anymore.

"Well played, I suppose," James said, but there was nothing pleasant in his tone. He sounded like he could kill Archibald.

"Yes. You can't always win, Abernathe," Archibald said with another of those sneers that made Emma's stomach turned. *This* was the man her father would have her marry. This...bastard. She could only imagine the hell her life would be if they had their way.

James's face had grown even harder. "You did all this just to get back at *me*?"

"You humiliated me," Archibald snapped, folding his arms. "In front of a party full of people, over some chit."

James took a long step forward. "So you wanted to swing on me and you wanted a bride, and you thought you got both in one fell swoop. But *you* don't know our news, Sir Archibald."

Sir Archibald blinked. "News?"

"Aye," James said, and now he slipped an arm around Emma. He drew her to his side, his fingers tightening at her ribcage, warmth threading through her entire body at the gentle, soothing touch. "Emma has already agreed to marry me."

Sir Archibald's face fell and he spun on Mr. Liston. "What?"

Liston held up his hands. "It's not my fault, I didn't know there had been arrangements made."

Sir Archibald gulped at air and faced James again. "You cannot thwart the desires of her father, Abernathe. You cannot subvert a contract made between us."

"*And* after I announced the arrangement with Sir Archibald publicly," Mr. Liston added weakly, clearly feeling trapped between two powerful men.

James squeezed Emma gently before he stepped away, staring down at Sir Archibald. The old man actually flinched, and she couldn't help her smile.

"I'm the *Duke of Abernathe*," James said softly. "With more power and money and influence than the two of you sorry lot put together. *I* am the Duke of Abernathe and I can do whatever the bloody hell I want. I'm marrying Emma Liston and there is *nothing* you can do about it."

Sir Archibald sputtered, then glared first at Mr. Liston before he turned his attention to Emma. His face was red, his eyes lit up with pure hatred. "No one humiliates me twice. This is *not* done."

He raced from the room just as James took another step toward him. Emma let out a wavering sigh and covered her face with her hands as emotion flooded her.

James had saved her. But at what cost?

Her father and mother didn't seem to care, though. Both stepped forward, and it was her father who spoke. "Well played, Abernathe! Obviously you are a far better match for Emma and we support it wholeheartedly."

"Wholeheartedly," Mrs. Liston mimicked as she turned her attention on Emma. "Oh, Emma, a duchess! You'll be a duchess. What a coup!"

Emma lowered her hands, staring at both of them. Her parents, the grasping twosome. A man who never stayed for any hard time in his life. A man who had apparently gambled with her future more than once. A man who took no responsibility for the damage he did.

And his wife, a woman who had depended upon Emma to save her rather than doing her duty as a mother. A woman who manipulated through tears and accusations. A woman who saw love as a weapon.

"How could you?" Emma whispered. Then her voice elevated. "How could you?"

"Well, that's a fine reaction," Mr. Liston responded, actually daring to look shocked. "I bring you not one husband but two, and you're angry with *me*?"

James lunged at him then. He caught him by the collar and hauled him toward the parlor door. He opened it and tossed him out, then turned toward Mrs. Liston. "You too," he growled.

She followed, sending Emma expectant and worried looks that were at last cut off when she stepped into the hallway and James slammed the door in her face.

He turned, and Emma looked up at him. She stared at his handsome face, the face of this man she loved. The man who would throw away the future he'd planned to protect her. A man who would certainly one day look at her with regret, and she bent her head.

He said nothing, but simply crossed the room to her and folded her into his arms. She sank into the touch, into the comfort he provided, digging her fingers into his back as he smoothed his hand along her hair and whispered empty platitudes. She let him for she didn't know how long, drinking in his strength and his warmth and his tenderness. But at last she opened her eyes and took the hardest step she'd ever taken.

The one away from him.

She would not be her mother. She would not destroy someone else to save herself.

"James, you do not know how much I appreciate your words in the breakfast room and your defense of me just now," she began, her voice trembling.

He made to step toward her, but she held up her hand to stop him. "Emma."

She shook her head. "Please let me finish, James. I—you cannot marry me."

He arched a brow. "Do I need to make the speech about being the Duke of Abernathe again, of getting to do whatever I want?"

He was teasing, but she didn't smile. This was too serious to allow him to make it less. She shook her head slowly. "There are a dozen reasons I am not fit to be your bride, James."

"A dozen?" he repeated. "I doubt that. Name them."

She huffed out a breath. "First, I am not anywhere close to your rank. Marrying me will link you to a minor viscountcy, and one that doesn't even acknowledge me as their family."

"I have always liked minor viscounts," James said. "And I like your grandfather, truth be told. Perhaps once we are wed, he can meet you and see that you are worthy of his attention. If he doesn't, then please refer to the speech I made about being the Duke of Abernathe and far more important than anyone else in the room."

"James, I have virtually no dowry," she said.

He looked around and she tracked his gaze. All around her were beautiful, expensive things. He finally looked back at her. "Do I look like I am hurting for funds?"

She shook her head. "Of course not, but—"

"No buts. That is two, Emma, two not very good reasons that I should not uphold what I vowed not only to your parents but to a room of incredibly gossipy ladies and lords."

She threw up her hand and paced away. "Then let us get into the meat of the problem. You could have anyone, James. Any beautiful woman in that room we just left or any other in the entire kingdom. I know what I am. I know that I am not the kind of woman that a man like you desires."

He made a soft sound in his throat and she turned to find him stalking across the room toward her. He caught her elbows and drew her up hard against him, then his mouth came down on hers. He kissed her deeply, passionately and thoroughly before he gently set her aside.

"You are a woman I very much desire, Emma Liston," he whispered, his voice suddenly husky. "So much so that I think I shall not be able to wait until you're my bride before I make you mine. I desire you completely. And there is no other woman in that room we just left or any other I've ever been in who has inspired such focused lust in me. Even when I didn't want to feel it. Next issue."

She blinked up at him, equally stunned by his words and by the fact that he seemed to mean them. He wanted her. Truly wanted her, and from her spinning head to her flexing toes and every inch of her tingling body between...she wanted him in return.

"Nothing else?"

"My parents are an embarrassment," she whispered, blinking back tears. "Marrying me won't stop my father from acting a fool or my mother from trying to manipulate more and more and more from you."

"You are not your parents," James said softly. "And you know that Meg and I both fully understand exactly what it means to have a parent...or two...who make one's life difficult. I would never judge *you* for that."

She bent her head, shocked that he could so easily dismiss every fear in her heart. Save one.

"Finally," she whispered, "My last objection to this is the most important one. And that is that you have made it abundantly clear to me and to everyone you care most about, that you do not wish to marry anyone. That you have plans for your future that don't include a bride or children."

He was quiet a moment, and her heart sank even though she couldn't read his handsome face to know what was inside of him. Finally he sighed. "My first response to you is that if this is your final objection, it is only your sixth and not the dozen I was promised."

"I'll think of more, I'm sure," she said.

He slid a finger beneath her chin and forced her to look up into his eyes. "Emma Liston, you may think of a hundred more and they will not change a thing about my intentions. You are right that I've always thought I would remain a bachelor, that I would avoid the duty my father found most important: to carry on his name and title. But I am not a child anymore. Some things are more important than a fit of pique. Saving you chief amongst them."

"Save me at your own peril," she whispered. "And with the knowledge that you will one day come to resent the options I took from you."

He grasped both her shoulders and squeezed gently. "We have become friends, haven't we?"

She nodded slowly. "Yes."

"And you want me?" he asked, his voice growing rough again and his pupils dilating.

She swallowed hard before she forced herself to nod again, this time without speaking a word.

He smiled faintly. "Then that is all I could hope for. To be with a friend who I desire sounds like a fine marriage, Emma. Anything else I am…I'm incapable of. So this will be enough for me."

She stared at him, feeling her heart break rather than soar. He would marry her. There was clearly no getting around that now—he would not allow her to escape it.

But he would never love her. He was making that perfectly clear. It was funny how disappointing that realization was. After all, she had never believed she would marry for love. At least not for many years.

But today it felt like a loss.

Perhaps because she already loved him. And she had a sneaking suspicion that marrying him would only make those feelings grow rather than fade over time. She would be in love alone.

"I announced our engagement in public, Emma, and thwarted your father's plans in the most dramatic way," he said, taking her hand. "And then you fainted. The stir caused by both our actions cannot be understated. Undoing it would only make things worse for both of us, but especially you. You would be in danger from Sir Archibald and your father even more than you were before."

"So you will not change your mind?" she whispered.

His gaze flickered away, and for a brief moment she thought

she saw hurt in his stare, but then it was gone. Buried, if it had ever existed.

"I *cannot*," he corrected her gently. "We are going to marry, Emma. And because I do not trust your father, I think we'd better make it sooner rather than later."

CHAPTER EIGHTEEN

James walked into the billiard room and straight to the sideboard, where he poured himself a full tumbler of scotch. He took a long sip, feeling the burn down his throat as he fought to find breath.

He was engaged. It was finished. Tonight it would be solidified completely when the planned ball was turned into an engagement celebration after some hasty arrangements from his sister.

He was *engaged.*

"Drink all that this early and you will be no good at the ball tonight."

James turned to find Graham, Simon, Sheffield, Brighthollow and Roseford entering the room. Simon reached behind him to shut the door and all five men simply stared at James with equally intense expressions on their face. The emotions were different, though. Graham and Simon both looked concerned, Brighthollow and Roseford looked horrified, and Sheffield was pale as paper.

"Well, don't all congratulate me at once," James muttered, setting aside the liquor.

"Do you wish to be congratulated?" Brighthollow asked, eyebrow arching.

James sighed. Hugh had never been a believer in love. He could be hard. And Roseford was little better. He believed in passion and nothing else. The two of them *would* be horrified that he'd been caught in a web by a lady, of course.

"I am marrying," he said, the words surprising him even though he'd been the one to ensure they were true. "It is tradition."

"Congratulations," Roseford said softly, but it didn't exactly sound sincere.

"I still don't fully understand how it happened," Simon said, stepping up to clap a hand on James's arm. "Meg was talking so fast when she found me, it took her the entire ride back to the estate just to make it clear."

Graham jerked his face toward Simon. "Meg?"

Simon didn't look at their friend, but kept his gaze trained on James. "Yes. Late this morning she found me riding around the estate to tell me the news."

Graham didn't look pleased at that, but he said nothing else about the matter except, "I'm not sure what there is to explain, Crestwood. James is marrying Miss Liston in order to save her from the unfortunate match her father made. What else is to be said?"

"I have to say, I never pegged you as the man to save a woman through marriage," Roseford chuckled. "That's more Simon's speed."

Simon ignored the playful jab, keeping his attention on his search of James's face. "Saving someone is well and good and noble. But the question to be asked is if you *want* to marry her. Do you?"

James felt like there was a fist in his stomach and it was opening, filling him up, stretching him uncomfortably. A great part of him considered marriage and wanted to bolt into the night and never return. Another part considered marriage with Emma and wanted to curl into her in a way that felt just as dangerous.

He wasn't certain which reaction was more terrifying.

"It is happening, and as quickly as I can arrange it," he said. "*Want* no longer comes into the equation."

"He is right," Sheffield said softly, and there was a wistful tone to his voice and to the expression on his face. "Even men like us, men with power, sometimes have little choice in our future. Society and situation dictate us all. It is the way of our world whether or not we wish to accept it."

"Jesus, Sheffield," Brighthollow said with a shake of his head. "Be a little more maudlin."

Sheffield glared at him, but then he smiled weakly at James. "I'm not trying to sound dire. The fact is, Miss Liston doesn't seem the worst sort you could marry. No one can pretend you don't seem to like her."

James bent his head. *Like* her. What a benign term for what boiled inside of him whenever he was within ten feet of Emma. It was need and want and passion, yes, and all those things he could have accepted and even reveled in.

But there was more than that physical attraction when he was with Emma. He did like her, but it was more complicated than that rather simple and childish feeling. He felt nervous around her. He felt…restless. He wanted to stand closer to her, he wanted to know more about her, he wanted to protect her, he wanted to show her things and places.

He sighed. "I do like her," he admitted.

"Well, that is better than many men of rank find in a bride," Graham said. "So we will celebrate with you."

Simon nodded and slipped to the sideboard to pour more of the scotch James had been guzzling upon their arrival. He handed glasses all around and then inclined his head toward Graham for the toast.

"To James," Graham said, holding James's stare evenly. "Our fearless leader, who will now fearlessly lead us all into this next phase of our lives. And to Emma, the only woman clever enough to catch him."

James smiled and the rest laughed before they raised their glasses in unison. "To James and Emma," they all repeated.

James drank again, this time slower in order to savor this moment a little longer. It was likely one of the last he would have as a bachelor.

Soon everything would change.

Emma stepped into the ballroom and felt every eye in the room swing to her. She took a long breath and tried to ignore their whispers and glances. She would have to become accustomed to it, it seemed. Certainly the Duchess of Abernathe would inspire such a response more often than plain Emma Liston ever had.

Especially since she was becoming Duchess of Abernathe under such trying circumstances.

"Some people get what they do not deserve," one woman sniffed loudly as Emma passed.

She stiffened at the slur as she continued walking through the room. Walking toward what, she did not know. She hadn't yet found James in the crowd and the girls along the wall would not meet her stare anymore.

Suddenly she felt an arm slide through hers and found Meg at her side, beaming with friendship and love for her, and Emma nearly buckled at it. Marrying Abernathe would make Meg her sister. She was very much looking forward to that.

"Smile," Meg said. "I have you now."

"It seems your family makes a habit of saving me," Emma said through a smile that hurt her cheeks.

Meg shrugged. "You saved us, too, I have not forgotten it. Perhaps that is what family does, save each other. It all evens out in the end, I think."

"I hope James believes the same," Emma sighed. "Though I cannot imagine my helping you once equals the sacrifice he is making on my behalf, no matter how kindly he makes it."

Meg turned toward her. "Don't make him a savior, Emma. His whole life he's been put up on a high shelf, the heir, the duke, the man who could do no wrong. That makes him a doll, not a man. And he is a man with flaws and faults and pains like any other. Bring him down to be a human with you, be patient with him as he figures this out. Whatever you do, don't stifle that you love him, even if you think that's what he wants."

Emma jolted. "L-love him?"

Meg arched a brow. "Will you deny that you love him?"

Emma sighed. "I suppose I could, but you are tenacious. I assume you would only browbeat the truth out of me."

Meg laughed. "I certainly would. Good, I'm glad I'm not seeing things. And I'm *glad* you love him. He's had little of that in his life, little of it he could depend upon. I want that for him." She gazed into the distance. "He's coming now, coming for you."

Emma's heart leapt and she smoothed her skirts reflexively. "What if I can't do this?" she whispered.

"You are stronger than you want to believe," Meg said softly, then turned her toward James as he took the last few steps toward her. "Now get what you deserve, Emma. Take it."

James smiled as he reached them. "Hello, Emma. Meg." Meg waved as she moved away and James blinked at her hasty exit. "Goodbye, Meg."

Emma looked up into his face, thinking of what Meg had just said to her. That he was a man, not anything less or more. Certainly, she was well aware of his maleness in this moment, but Meg meant something different.

"Should we dance?" she blurted out.

He grinned. "Aren't I meant to ask you that?"

She shrugged one shoulder. "We've broken with all other tradition in the past twenty-four hours—why not destroy it all?"

He bowed slightly. "I would very much like to dance with you, Miss Liston."

He reached out and she stared as she placed her smaller hand in his. She was wearing gloves, though he was not, but she felt the warmth of his touch regardless. She felt the strength of his hand as he guided her onto the dancefloor. To her surprise, everyone else fell away, leaving them a space as the music began and he spun her into the steps.

"Why are they backing up?" she whispered.

"It is our first dance as an engaged couple," he murmured in return, his gaze never leaving her. "I suppose they are sizing up the match."

She shivered slightly. "Then should we give them a show?"

His smile fell and there was something intense and serious in his gaze. "There are many things that are a show, Emma. But not this moment. Don't worry about them, just look at me and enjoy this."

"It's hard to enjoy it when I know the cost," she insisted.

He shook his head. "I have not made myself clear. There is no cost. Tonight, in this moment, I am right where I want to be."

She felt her lips part as joy and hope filled her. She had spent so very long telling herself that a man like this wouldn't want her, couldn't truly like her, but now she felt the warmth of him. And it was just for her.

"So am I," she said, eliciting another grin from him as he held her hand tighter and whirled her around again and again, until all she could focus on was that she was his. Somehow, against all odds, she would be his.

James stood in the shadow of a door in the quiet hallway, staring at Emma's chamber across the way. She was inside, and despite the late hour, she was not alone. He could occasionally hear an eruption of giggles from the room, both Emma's and Meg's.

He smiled at the sound. He was not only bringing a bride into his home, but a sister for Meg. After a lifetime surrounded by him and his friends, he could well imagine she was looking forward to female company in the house for as long as she would remain there before her own wedding to Graham.

The chamber door opened and Meg stepped out. "Goodnight, Emma," she whispered.

"Goodnight," he heard in the distance, and his heart throbbed with the sound.

Meg was smiling as she closed Emma's door behind herself and strolled off down the hall, away from the guest quarters, back toward the family rooms. When he heard her door open and shut, he drew in a long breath and walked to Emma's door.

There was a moment when he stood there, staring at the barrier that stood between him and what he wanted. He could turn away from it, from her and go back to his room. Self-pleasure was good. He could relieve his desire that way, certainly.

But he didn't want to. What he wanted was behind this door.

He lifted his hand and knocked gently. There was a moment when he heard rustling and then footsteps across the floor.

"Meg, did you forget—" she began as she yanked the door open. When she saw him standing there, she gasped. "—something?"

He looked at her. She was already clad in a night rail and a robe. Her dark hair was down around her shoulders, a mass of shining brown curls with little streaks of blond hidden within them.

And there would be no turning away tonight.

"I am not Meg," he whispered as he reached for her. "But I did forget something. This."

He leaned in and kissed her. For a moment she seemed surprised, but then she lifted up, her arms coming around his neck as she made a soft sound of needy pleasure in the back of her throat. He pushed her into the chamber and shut the door behind them, reaching back to turn the key before he fully focused on tasting her.

"How can you be so sweet?" he murmured, drawing back just a fraction and feeling the heat of her breath on his lips. "I never even liked sweets until you."

She shivered and he tightened his embrace around her. She looked up at him, eyes wide. "Why did you come here, James?"

"To your room?" he asked. She nodded slowly, and he

smiled. "Why do you think?"

She swallowed hard, the action making her throat work. Making him want to trace the path of that action with his tongue until she lifted and moaned against him.

"Did you come here to…to…I don't know what to call it," she said with a dark blush that started in her cheeks and cascaded down her flesh until it disappeared beneath the neckline of her robe, creating yet another trail for his tongue.

"I came here," he said, reaching down to begin to loosen the knot of her dressing gown. "Because until now I had to be prudent. I had to resist what I wanted. But now we're engaged. In a very short time, you will be mine in the eyes of God. The eyes of the law. The eyes of everyone we know and love. Because of that I have nothing else stopping me from making love to you, Emma."

Her eyes went wide, and he could see her struggling with that idea.

"Nothing stopping me unless you don't want me to do this," he clarified.

"I have a few qu-questions," she stammered.

"Of course you do," he said with a laugh. "Anything."

"I know very little about this. My mother says you must bear it, but when you touched me before it was wonderful. Will it be like that?"

He bit back a curse at her utter innocence. It was both alluring and terrifying. He would have to keep it at the top of his mind at all times now, so that he wouldn't frighten or hurt her.

"It will be like that," he promised. "And even better. But there will be a little pain when I first…penetrate you."

She nodded. "That must be the bearing part she discussed. The pain."

He smiled. "The pain only happens the first time, Emma. And if I'm doing my job right, there won't be any bearing. There will only be wanting and pleasure for both of us."

She seemed to ponder that a moment, then she dropped her hands to where his were, still tangled in the loops of her robe.

She gently pushed them aside and unknotted the fabric before she shrugged out of it and let it fall to the floor.

CHAPTER NINETEEN

Emma watched as James tracked her robe falling away and then stared at her in her flimsy night rail. No man had ever seen her so revealed, and she fought every instinct inside herself to cover up beneath his regard.

"What do I do?" she asked, voice shaking.

He lifted his gaze from her body to her face and shook his head. "Nothing. Tonight is about you. You lay back and let me pleasure you."

Her entire body quivered at those words and the dark, seductive tone with which he said them. Suddenly she wanted more, she wanted everything he had to give. She wanted everything he had been holding back in their unconventional "courtship".

He slid a hand across her shoulder, gliding his fingers beneath the strap of her shift. His hands were warm and slightly rough as he dragged the strap down her arm, and the left side of her nightgown dropped forward.

She shivered as the warm air in her chamber touched her skin. Only her face felt hot in that moment, like her cheeks were actually on fire.

James's breath was ragged now as he stared at her. He lifted his hand, and she was shocked to find it trembled slightly as he covered her breast.

Sensation mobbed her, more powerful than anything she'd

ever felt before, even when he'd made her shatter in the past. His bare skin against her bare skin was shocking and perfect, as if it was always meant to be like this. Like she'd been missing some piece of herself and now she'd found it in the gentle touch of his fingers.

"You are wonderful," he promised as he slid the opposite strap of her gown down. The entire contraption pooled at her feet, and suddenly she was very naked before him.

She ducked her head, and this time she couldn't stop herself from covering her breasts with one arm and the place between her legs with her opposite hand.

"You needn't be shy," he said, taking her hand and drawing it away so her breasts were bare again. "I will be your husband in a few days and you will grow accustomed to my..."

"Regard?" she asked when he didn't finish the sentence.

"Obsession," he said with a low chuckle. "Right now it feels more like obsession when I look at you."

"How is that possible?" she squeaked out. "I am not the kind of woman who inspires such things in men. I never have been."

His expression softened and he stepped toward her, sliding a hand across her jawline and into her hair. "Men were blind or sleeping. I'm glad they were. It left you there, waiting, when I finally woke up."

She swallowed past the lump in her throat. When he looked at her like he did right now, she could almost believe that he wanted her. That their ruse could somehow have truly transformed to something real for him as much as it had for her.

Even if that real thing was just the desire that now pulsed in the room. She would take it.

She lifted on her tiptoes and wound her arms around his neck. Her breasts flattened against his jacket and the rough fabric abraded the sensitive nipples. She tipped her head back with a gasp at the unexpected sensations rushing through her body, and he let out a needy moan.

"You are incredibly responsive," he said, almost in awe.

"And I intend to use that to my benefit."

Without another word, he swept his arm beneath her bare legs and carried her to her bed. He deposited her on top of the coverlet, and as she settled back on the pillows he shrugged out of his jacket and then went to work on the shirt beneath.

She sat up on her elbows to watch him, fascinated by the slow reveal of masculine flesh covering muscle and bone. When he tugged the item off his head, she caught her breath. He was…perfect. Utterly perfect, like the statues of Greek gods that dotted the gardens of country homes all over England.

Those men were carved of stone, though. This one was very real. She reached out and touched his chest. He was warm, his muscles rippled beneath her fingertips, and he sucked in a ragged breath that made her jerk her hand away.

"I'm sorry," she said.

"Do it again," he ordered, the smoky darkness of his tone enough to make that empty place between her legs tingle and throb.

She met his gaze and slowly followed his order, rising up to press a hand to his chest once more.

"Goddamn, but you test me," he growled. "And make me want to do things to you…"

Her eyes widened. "Do things?" she repeated.

"Oh yes," he said as he leaned down, placing one hand on either side of her head. "Tonight I will be tender with you, gentle, because you deserve that. But one day you will crave all the wicked things that race through my mind when I touch you."

She found herself smiling even though she didn't fully understand what he meant. Already she craved him. Already she would have given anything he asked, just to belong to him.

Tonight, for just a little while, she *would* belong to him.

He leaned into the edge of the mattress, his upper body pushing her back against the pillows as he ducked his head to kiss her once more. Her grip tightened against his shoulders and her breath grew ragged as he drove his tongue between her lips and tasted her with increasing urgency.

Finally he pulled away, panting as he stared down at her. Without breaking the stare, he straightened, unfastened his trousers and let them fall.

She sat up slightly, staring at the naked body of this man she loved and desired.

She'd never seen a naked man before, except in a few paintings. Certainly a lady like herself wasn't supposed to see a naked man until her wedding night. And not even then, if some rumors were to be believed.

But James stood before her, every inch of him muscled and toned. That thing between his legs looked impossibly hard and big and curved and…terrifying. And yet enticing. She wanted to push him away, but also trace her finger along his length.

"Your eyes are big as saucers," he said softly.

Those words made her jerk her attention away from his body and up to his face. "I just haven't…I never…I don't know what to do."

"I already told you," he said with a half-smile. "Nothing. *I* know what to do."

She swallowed. "Then tell me. Tell me what that is, because right now I am frankly…petrified."

He laughed softly. "That won't do. Petrified won't do at all. What I'm going to do, Emma, is open your legs, like I have when I've touched you, tasted you, and I'm going to ready you for me by doing those same things you've liked before."

She shivered with desire at that news, but it couldn't erase her anxiety about the unknown that would follow. "And then?"

"And then," he said, leaning over her, covering her body as he climbed onto the bed. "When you are slick and hot and needy, I will place my cock inside of you."

"Cock," she repeated on the barest of breath.

"Yes," he said, reaching up to take her hand and lowering it so she could touch him intimately. "This is my cock. And it was made to fill you, Emma."

"It seems rather big for that purpose," she argued as she slid her fingers over him. He was so hard and yet the skin was so soft.

He laughed again, but his tone was strangled as he gasped out, "You flatter. But I assure you it isn't. You were made to take it. Made to stretch to accommodate it. I won't lie and tell you that the first time there won't be pain. But I will make sure there is also pleasure. This time and every time afterward. Because when your body shakes and trembles, when you feel needy and hot when I touch you, it is *this* that you crave." He pushed himself up into her hand and she gasped. "This joining of our bodies will make us one more than any vow we ever take in the future."

She stared at him as he said all those words, said them with passion, said them without breaking his gaze from hers. And her fear faded, replaced by a pulsing desire to surrender to him. Fully.

She found herself nodding and he ducked his head. This time he didn't kiss her mouth, though, but her throat, tracing the column of it with delicate nips and strokes. She released his cock and placed her hands on his shoulders, her fingers tightening against the muscles there as he trailed lower, gliding his lips across her collarbone, her chest, and ultimately he covered one nipple with his mouth.

She arched with a gasp of pleasure as he began to tug the nipple with his lips, lick and lave it with his rough tongue. She slid her fingers through his hair, holding him there as she turned her head into the pillow and grunted out pleasure and desire.

He lifted his eyes as he continued to torment her, the dark intensity there forcing her to stay with him, to watch him as he touched her in ways she had never imagined were possible and yet sang to her in some ancient language she understood perfectly.

Her body responded to him of its own accord. Her legs went limp and opened slightly beneath him, her nipples pebbled and throbbed, her back arched and tiny cries escaped her lips as she surrendered inch by inch, moment by moment.

He shifted to her opposite breast, drawing the same pleasure there. Her sex was getting wet as he performed his act and her body writhed beneath him. She had never felt anything like it, not even in all the times he had so scandalously touched her. This was more...focused somehow. More purposeful.

But of course it would be. This was leading to a claiming, a final act that would change her body and her soul, that would change everything between them forever.

And as frightening as that was, she didn't fight it. She practically purred as he traced his hand down her bare side and then slid his fingers between their bodies. He found her sex, continuing to suckle at her breast as he spread her folds open and smoothed the wetness of her body across the tingling entrance there.

He popped his mouth free. "You are so wet, Emma. So ready. And I want you so much. But I need to know that you want me to do this tonight. Once I do, there will be no going back. No escape. So you must look at me and tell me that you want me."

She swallowed hard. This was her final chance to end the madness that was building and swirling inside of her. The last chance to walk away from him.

But she didn't want to do that. Not tonight. Not ever.

She reached up and cupped his cheeks. She met his eyes, holding him as steady as she could manage when her world was spinning wildly.

"I'm yours, James," she whispered. "And I want you."

He let out a sigh that felt like it held the relief of a thousand lives in it. Then he stared down into her eyes as he positioned himself differently. She felt the hardness of him, of his cock, pressed at that slick spot between her trembling legs. She found herself lifting into him without meaning to do so, and then he was pressing inside.

"Oh God," he groaned as the tip of him entered her. "You are perfect."

She whimpered a response because there were no longer words in her head. There was just this animal act between them that she wanted and feared in equal measure.

He took another inch, and there was the pain he had told her about, a quick tearing that made her suck in her breath and dig her fingernails into his shoulders.

"I know," he murmured, "I know, I'm sorry. But I promise you that is the end of it, Emma. It will never hurt again."

She nodded slowly, praying he was right and knowing he might not be. He moved forward, taking her further and further until she felt certain there was no space left in her body for him. When he had taken her to the hilt, he stopped and held still inside her.

She stared up at him in wonder, and he smiled. "What is that look for?"

"You told me I was made to accept you," she said with a shake of her head. "I just didn't believe you."

He leaned in to kiss her gently. "When it comes to this, I would never lie to you, Emma. And now I can't wait anymore. I have to have you, really have you."

He thrust as he said the last word, and she gasped at the thick slide of him inside her clenching body. It was such a strange sensation, foreign but also oddly natural. He didn't belong where he was, and yet each time he moved inside of her, it felt more and more right.

And then he shifted his hips in a slow circle and she froze. This was no longer odd, it was...good. So good. Pleasure rocked through her as he circled again, grinding his pelvis against hers and eliciting a harsh moan from her lips.

"That's right," he whispered. "That's what I want, Emma. I want your pleasure. I want to make you shake with it."

She lifted against him, and now it was he who made a harsh sound of pleasure. She smiled. It seemed for once she might just have as much power as he did.

They began to move together, their eyes locked as she lifted into him, as he drove into her. The thrusts came harder and faster now, and her body reacted with blissful sensation as the pleasure he created mounted, increasing as his neck strained and his eyes glazed.

And then release hit her, in waves that were far more intense than anything he had drawn from her before. She clung to him, burying her mouth against his naked shoulder so the household wouldn't be brought down by the cries of her release.

He thrust through it all, demanding more, taking more, and finally he let out her name in a pleading cry and she felt heat fill her. The heat of *him*, the heat of his release. He collapsed down over her, his breath ragged as he held her tight, smoothing his hands over her hair, her back, her shoulders, while he rolled to his side and pulled her flush against him.

How long they lay like that, she had no idea. All she knew was that she felt warm, safe, protected like she never had in her entire life. When James's arms were around her, it was a cocoon where no evil could penetrate. And she loved him all the more for creating that little haven of safety, even if it was only in her mind.

He leaned down and kissed her temple before he separated their still entangled bodies and got to his feet. She watched him as he bent, gloriously comfortable in his nakedness as he dressed.

"You have to go?" she asked, hating the faint desperation in her question.

He glanced at her over his shoulder. "I must. Since we are to wed, the scandal if we were caught wouldn't be as bad as it would have been a day ago, but it is not the way I want your life as Duchess of Abernathe to start. So I *must* go."

He was still tucking his shirt into his trousers when he turned back to her. He looked at her, that heated stare flitting from her head to her toes, and shook his head. "Amazing," he muttered.

"What's that?" she asked softly.

He leaned in and kissed her once more. "That the wanting doesn't fade with you," he explained. He brushed his nose back and forth against hers. "And now you are truly mine. Now there is no going back."

He kissed her cheek once more, grinned at her and departed her bedroom. Once he was gone, she got to her own feet and picked up her discarded night rail. But as she slid it over her head, she caught her breath, not with pleasure, but with pain. Disappointment.

When he'd said there was no going back, she had seen something in his eyes. Something that had flared there in worry, in upset.

He had made love to her tonight, and she'd had such hopes that it meant a new beginning for them. A start where she might one day earn the same love from him that *she* felt.

Only now she saw the truth. He'd come to her not just because there was desire between them that could not be denied. He'd come because he needed a reason why he couldn't go back on his word. He had to ruin her so there would be no opportunity to escape the promise he'd made.

She walked to the window and stared into the darkness outside. He had said she was his. And she was.

But he wasn't hers. And she feared he might never be.

CHAPTER TWENTY

James stood on the parapet overlooking the garden below. In the distance he could see dozens of servants arranging chairs, decorating the gazebo, hustling with flowers and ribbon.

They were preparing the space where he would marry Emma in…he glanced down at his pocket watch…two hours.

He sighed. Everything in the past week and a half had flown by. He'd had a special license to arrange, there had been seamstresses coming and going, looking harried and displeased, despite how much he was paying them to swiftly prepare a gown for his future wife. And there had still been his country party to lord over. Only now it was a wedding party, and the tone of it all had shifted significantly.

The one thing there had not been time for, it seemed, was a moment alone with Emma. He frowned at that thought. He'd been dreaming about making love to her, but she never seemed to be alone anymore. She had even asked Meg to stay in her room with her until their wedding night, thwarting his attempts to join her as he had before.

She was avoiding him.

"Your Grace?"

He turned and stifled a groan at the person who had interrupted him. Mrs. Liston, his future mother-in-law, now stood at the terrace door. She and her husband had *not* been avoiding him since the engagement, unfortunately. He'd had the distinct displeasure of spending a great deal of time with them. He had been asked for money, time, introductions, even a cottage on his estate. Never directly, of course, always in a roundabout way that made it seem like their concern was only for Emma.

Oh yes, he had become very familiar with their grasping ways.

"Mrs. Liston," he said, his tone cool. "You are lovely, as always."

She glanced down at her gown with a titter. "I would have had a new gown made—mother of the bride, you know—but there was no time. Not that I am complaining."

His lips thinned as he thought of her words on the terrace so many nights ago. He'd overheard her plotting with Emma to "catch" him. Emma had refused, though it had all turned out exactly as this woman had desired.

And she looked rather proud of it.

When he didn't say anything, she moved forward. "I would like to talk to you about my daughter's future."

He frowned. "As we have discussed before, your daughter's future is taken care of, Mrs. Liston. She will want for nothing ever again." She shifted slightly, and James lifted both eyebrows. It seemed they were done dancing around what this woman wanted. She was ready to be more direct. "Ah, I see. You really mean you wish to speak to me about *your* future."

She nodded and moved closer to him. "Mine and my husband's."

James tightened his fists at his sides. Any time he spent with his future father-in-law was a continuing exercise in self-control. Knowing what Mr. Liston had done to Emma, what he had *tried* to do, it made James want to destroy the man.

And now her mother came, asking for a boon for him. For herself.

"I want to make something very clear, Mrs. Liston," he said softly. "I shall give Emma whatever she desires for the rest of her life. I shall happily do so, for I know her character. I know that she deserves no less. But as for your husband, when this wedding is over, I would not be sorry to never see him again."

Mrs. Liston's lips parted and her eyes went wide. "Your Grace—"

He held up a hand to stop her talking. "*Enough.* I do not understand you. How you can know exactly what he is, how you can hear what he did to your daughter, the future he would have created for her in order to save himself, and still coo into his ear like you are newlyweds?"

Dark color flooded her cheeks and she turned away from him suddenly. "I—" she began. "He—he has promised to change. He has sworn that now that Emma is settled, he will also alter his ways. He will come to London with me, stay in our home there. We will only need a bit of help and he—"

"How did Emma grow up to be so very clever?" James interrupted with a shake of his head. "If you are so foolish as to believe those lies."

"They are not lies, Your Grace," she snapped, facing him again, her arms folded in defiance and her eyes filled with tears.

"How many times has he told you the very same thing?" he whispered. "How many times has he promised you diamonds and pearls, fidelity and calm?"

Her expression told him everything he wanted to hear and he shook his head slowly. "Emma cares for you, despite all you have allowed during her life. And if she would like to support you, I will never argue against it. But her father…that man will *never* receive a penny from my purse. And I will do *everything* in my power to make sure he never hurts her again. Take a little advice, Mrs. Liston, from someone who knows it all too well. People do not change. And you will only be disappointed if you believe your husband's tales one more time."

She stared at him, her hands clenched at her sides and her bottom lip trembling. In that moment, he saw Emma in her. Emma in twenty years, if she was denied safety and security…love.

He could give her the first two, but the last? Would

marrying him doom her as much as marrying Sir Archibald would have done?

He shook off the troubling question as Mrs. Liston stepped up to him. "You owe us," she whispered.

He arched a brow. "I owe *Emma*. Everything else is optional."

She huffed out her breath and raced from the balcony back into the house, leaving James alone again. He stared off into the distance once more. The servants were almost finished with their preparations for his wedding.

And now he did not know how to proceed with Emma once she was truly his. Because the idea of anyone's happiness belonging to him—or worse, his happiness belonging to someone else—was terrifying.

Emma hardly recognized the woman who stood looking at her in her mirror. Meg's seamstress had done wonders in a short amount of time, creating an exquisite gown stitched through with sparkling silver thread and a finely braided bodice. Her hair had been twisted, curled and piled in a beautiful fashion. Her cheeks had been pinched, her lips very lightly rouged, despite the naughtiness of that action.

She looked…different.

She *almost* looked like a duchess should.

"You are gorgeous," Meg said, leaning in to kiss Emma's cheek. "My brother will be enraptured!"

Emma bent her head. Enrapture James? That seemed almost impossible. He was marrying her out of duty, out of some sense that he had to save her. Soon enough whatever desire he felt for her would fade, and they would be left with…

Resentment. Perhaps one day even hatred.

She shivered, and Meg rubbed her bare arms gently. "Are you cold?"

"No," Emma said, covering her friend's hand. "Not cold. Thank you."

The door to her chamber opened and her mother stepped in. Emma rose to her feet as she stared at Mrs. Liston's drawn face. She was upset, that was clear. Dread rose up in Emma's chest, washing away any other good emotion she might have felt as she wondered in terror what her father might have done now.

"May I have a moment with my mother?" she said, smiling at Sally and Meg.

"Of course," Meg said, and turned to the maid. "Sally, you *must* talk to my maid. I would someday love to have my hair styled as you did Emma's. It is perfect."

They exited the room together, and Meg shut the door as they did so, leaving Emma alone with her mother. She moved toward her a step. "What is it?"

Her mother shook her head. "Awful man. You don't even know, Emma!"

Emma drew in long breaths and tried to keep her voice calm as she whispered, "What did he do? What did Father do now?"

"Your father?" Mrs. Liston burst out with an angry cackle. "No, it wasn't him who upset me."

Emma blinked in confusion. "Then who?"

"That future husband of yours," Mrs. Liston ground out. "Do you know he dared to say he would not support your father? He claims Harold doesn't deserve it after what he did to you. What he did? Well, he's the reason you're marrying a duke at all, isn't he?"

"Because he forced James's hand when he lost me in a bet?" Emma barked. "How wonderful of him, yes."

"Don't be impertinent," her mother snapped. "He saved you, in a roundabout way. But Abernathe is *insistent* that he shall not spare a farthing for your poor father."

Emma swallowed. Her mother meant for her to be upset by this knowledge, but she was creating an opposite reaction. As she stood there, listening to her mother rail about James's set down of her father, she felt...*protected*. Like she had finally found the champion she had prayed for all her life.

"My *poor* father," she repeated softly. "Is that what you have convinced yourself he is, a victim in all this?"

Her mother's eyes narrowed. "You may be a future duchess, but you still owe him respect. He's your father."

"Hardly," Emma said softly. "He has been in and out of my life for decades, Mama. And yours, for heaven's sake. Not a week ago, you were agonizing over him reappearing and destroying our lives. Now you speak of him like he is a saint."

Her mother shifted. "You don't understand love, Emma. If you did, you would know what I go through, what I must accept."

Emma turned away. She did understand love. She loved James—there was no longer any denying that. But she didn't want the life she had watched her mother live. One where she feared and longed for a man in equal measure. One where she was forced to forgive all transgressions out of some desperate hope for crumbs of his affection.

"You make the life you live, Mama," she said. "And so must I." She turned back. "If James does not wish to support Father, then…I do not question his decision."

Her mother's face crumpled and her hands clenched at her sides. "Ungrateful wretch," she hissed out before she spun around and raced from the room.

Emma leaned her hands against the closest table, her eyes stinging with tears, her body trembling after the confrontation she'd just had with her mother. The one that felt like it had been coming for a lifetime.

She wanted to curl up and cry. She wanted to run away from the pain in her heart. But mostly, she wanted to find James. For his comfort and his support, yes, but also because she knew what she needed to do. She knew what she needed to risk.

And if she didn't risk it now, she might never have another chance.

She straightened up and smoothed her gown, then walked from the chamber. She moved through the hallways, hearing talk and laughter from behind the doors in the guest quarters, smiling at the servants who now looked at her with new deference as their future mistress.

As she came down the staircase, Grimble was at the bottom. The butler had a long list and he was discussing it with a footman, but he waved the man off as she exited the stairs.

"Miss Liston," he said, his tone and expression warm. "Is there something I can do for you?"

"James," she breathed. "Abernathe. Where is he?"

The butler seemed slightly taken aback by her question, or perhaps it was her expression when she asked it, for she was certain she looked as troubled as she felt.

"His Grace is on the terrace," he said slowly.

"Thank you, Grimble," she said as she nodded. Her heart rate increased as she turned toward the back of the house, where she could join her future husband. Her legs and hands trembled as she entered a chamber and made for the French doors there. She pushed them open and looked down the terrace for the man she loved.

She found him immediately. But he wasn't alone. James stood ten feet away, his back to her…with a beautiful woman standing across from him. She squinted to see better and drew in a breath. It was the Countess of Montague, a lady everyone knew was open with her favors. She'd seen them talk before at the party, just in passing. But *this* was not a passing conversation. Lady Montague was leaning into James, her hand boldly lifted to his chest.

Emma watched them together, her hands shaking at her sides and tears stinging her eyes. James smiled at the other woman, and her heart broke as she turned away. Walked back into the house, back through to the foyer. Grimble said her name, but she ignored him as she exited the house and hurried down the path that took her from the house, toward the stables.

She walked for a short time, her breath ragged and her mind spinning. Had she seen James doing something wrong? Not exactly. He'd been talking to one of his guests. A female guest, yes, but she could certainly not expect him to never speak to another woman again just because he was marrying her.

It was the intimacy of the discussion that broke her. In that moment, she'd seen a glimpse of her potential future. She did not want to be like her mother, loving a man who didn't return the feelings, waiting for him to grace her with any kind of attention. She couldn't spend her life like that.

She turned a corner toward the stables, uncertain of her next step. Did she go back and confront James? Did she pretend this hadn't happened and move forward with the union, despite her questions?

Did she run away?

She stopped in the middle of the path as she tried to regain her composure.

"Well, well, well."

She turned at the snide voice coming from behind her. Who she saw there made her heart almost stop.

"S-Sir Archibald," she breathed, backing away from the man.

He stepped forward an equal distance, keeping her within arm's length. She stared at him, for he didn't look like the man who had expressed interest in her just a short time before. His hair was messy, his face red, like he'd been drinking, and his eyes were glassy.

"What is wrong with you?" she whispered.

He tilted his head as if confused by her question. "Wrong with *me*? Aside from the abject humiliation brought down on me by *your duke*?"

She shivered at the harsh and shrill tone of his voice. "What humiliation is that, Sir Archibald? Surely you never really wanted *me*. You hardly know me, and I could not be considered a catch based on my family and my lack of funds."

He arched a brow at her harsh self-assessment. "Perhaps not, but I had made my claim. Your father had approved the match. Abernathe should not have so publicly denied me. Now I am the laughingstock of the shire. Everyone whispers when

197

they see me, they laugh behind their hands. That shall not stand."

She caught her breath, for she saw the dangerous light of his stare. "What—what are you going to do?"

"Take what's his," he said softly. "To even the score."

He moved forward again and Emma yelped in terror as she swung out at him wildly. Her nails raked his cheek, leaving a swollen welt, and he growled out pain and increased anger.

"You have fight," he said, pushing forward. She slid along the wall, watching for a chance for escape, but wherever she moved, he followed. "I like fight."

Her heart throbbed. He was herding her toward the dark, empty stalls at the back of the big room. She let out a scream and he jumped, tackling her at last. Her shoulder hit the corner of one of the stalls and a burst of pain ripped through her.

He covered her mouth with his palm. "Hush now, no one is coming for you. Save all that noise for later."

She struggled, but he was surprisingly strong for a man of his years. In that moment she realized she was trapped. She was caught. And he was right—there was no one coming to help her.

CHAPTER TWENTY-ONE

James looked at the beautiful woman standing across from him, her slender hand touching his chest. There was no denying Lady Montague was charming and the tales of her sexual prowess were well known. Once upon a time, he might have been taken in by her, but now he stared down at her and felt...nothing.

He didn't want a dalliance with a skilled and jaded lover. He didn't want a mistress, as Lady Montague had just offered to become in no uncertain terms. It turned out he only wanted Emma.

"You are quiet, Abernathe," Lady Montague purred. "I am shocked you don't have a more immediate response to my...*suggestion*. After all, a discreet affair is common in our circles. I *know* you have indulged before, as have I. And I think we could be...good together."

He stepped away, forcing her hand to drop to her side. "I appreciate the offer, my lady. And perhaps you are correct that we *could* find pleasure together. But I am about to be married and I..." He shook his head at what he was about to say. "I intend to be faithful to my wife."

Lady Montague wrinkled her brow. "*Faithful?*" she repeated, like she didn't understand the word. "Truly?"

"Yes."

She stared at him for a long moment, then shrugged. "You

are a singular creature then, Your Grace. And Miss Liston is…lucky to have inspired such fealty. It is uncommon enough."

He nodded, for he knew that to be true. He just hadn't known he wanted to be one of the few in their circles who remained true to his bride until he had been offered a chance to be something else.

"Excuse me, my lady," he said with a gentle motion that could only encourage her to leave him. "I have much to prepare in this last hour before my wedding."

She nodded with a smile that didn't reach her eyes. "Indeed. Good afternoon, Your Grace."

He turned and left her, heading back into the house. He strode though the hallway toward the stairs, determined to find his fiancée. Though he had no idea what he would say to her when he did.

He passed through the foyer, turning to go up the stairway, when Grimble stepped up to the bottom of the stairs. "Your Grace?"

He heard the tension in his butler's tone and looked at him, even though he wanted to just rush up and find Emma in that moment. This sudden wedding had put a strain on his staff, and he owed them his attention. "Yes?"

"Sir, I'm sorry to interrupt, I know you have much to prepare, but…" The butler shifted. "I thought you should know that Miss Liston was looking for you earlier."

"Emma?" James asked, his pulse leaping. "Where?"

"She went out to the terrace to talk to you just moments ago," Grimble said. "But within a very short time, she came hurrying back through the house and went out the front."

James drew back. If Emma had come out on the terrace recently, she had not spoken to him. Of course, he had been preoccupied with Lady Montague.

His stomach dropped. If Emma had seen him with the lady, with her hand against his chest, she might have thought…

"Damn it," he muttered. "Out the front, you said?"

"Yes," Grimble said. "I watched her go toward the stables,

but the bend in the path prevented my being able to track her much further than that."

James rushed past him, out the door and down the same path Emma had apparently taken a few moments before. His head spun as he rushed to find her. After everything she'd been through, everything she'd watched her mother endure with her wayward father, if she'd seen him with Lady Montague, no one could blame her for expecting the worst.

Especially since she believed James was marrying her only out of some sense of honor or duty. But the fact was, it was much more than that.

Much, much more. Only he'd never told her that. He'd hardly allowed himself to acknowledge it in his own heart, let alone confess it to her or anyone else. Bearing his heart had never ended well for him, and so here he was, chasing after a woman whom he had likely hurt without meaning to.

And that meant a great deal to him. More than it should have.

"No!"

James froze as he approached the stable, for he had heard the sharp cry of a woman's voice within. Emma's voice.

He broke into a run, racing toward the stable at double time as he heard a truncated second scream. He rounded the corner into the still stable, his gaze darting from one side of the large space to the next. And there, in the far corner, in the shadowy darkness, he saw Emma. She was leaning back, tugging hard against a man's hand, a man's hand that gripped her wrist. The blackguard was obviously working to pull her into an empty stall.

James rushed forward. "Stop!" he called out.

Whoever was holding Emma released her and she staggered backward, nearly depositing herself on the dusty stable floor. James pulled her behind him and looked down into the stall to see who her attacker was.

His eyes went wide as he saw Sir Archibald in the narrow space. The older man's face was pale as paper and his lips trembled as he stared up at James. "Abernathe," he breathed.

James let him say nothing else before he threw a punch that connected squarely with Sir Archibald's jaw. Sir Archibald fell backward, colliding with the wall of the stable and letting out a pained grunt.

"What the hell are you doing here?" James asked, though he could see exactly what the man's intentions were. His clothing was in disarray, his shirt loose and untucked from his trousers.

That he had intended to harm Emma made James want to kill him.

He might have, but Emma wrapped a hand around his forearm, forcing him to look back at her. "James," she said softly.

He looked down into her tear-streaked face and caught his breath. Disheveled as she now was, she was also beautiful in her wedding gown.

"Did he hurt you?" he asked, reaching out to trace her jaw with his finger. "Did he touch you?"

"No," she reassured him. "Not yet. You stopped him."

He caught his breath. There were bruises on her wrist, faint but there. He lifted her hand up. "Emma…"

"I'm not hurt," she whispered, though her trembling voice said that was a lie. "I'm not hurt."

He spun back to face Sir Archibald, anger coloring his vision, but found that the man had snuck past him as he tended to Emma. Now he was running out the stable as fast as his legs could carry him. James rushed after him in time to see the bastard swing up on his horse and fly off toward the estate gates.

"I will see you dead if you come near her again!" James shouted, certain the wind carried his angry words to the hunched back of his enemy.

He turned back and reentered the stable. Back at the stall where Emma had been attacked, she leaned against the wall, her face pale and drawn. His heart clenched at her expression. At her pain.

"I will ride after him," he murmured, smoothing an errant lock of hair from her cheek. "I will *kill* him for what he tried to do."

"No," Emma said, stepping forward to clutch his arm. "James, you know what would happen if you did something like that. You could be transported or hanged. Even if you weren't, the scandal would destroy you. Destroy Meg. I am not worth that."

He stared at her. She believed what she said. Of course she would, after the life she'd led. And suddenly he wanted to give her so much more than she had already experienced. He wanted to give her everything. Everything he had and was. More importantly, he wanted to give her everything he could be but hadn't yet become.

He wanted to be better for her.

"You are worth far more," he said softly.

"I don't want to lose you," she said, forming each word succinctly. "Please don't follow him."

His ground his teeth. The idea of Archibald getting away after what he'd tried to do was disgusting. He would only hurt someone else. Or perhaps even come after Emma again in his vengeful state.

"I'll have Graham take care of it," he said at last. "When we return to London, he can monitor Sir Archibald. I'm sure he'll find help in that task from plenty of our friends."

She nodded. "Yes. Then you'll know if he has designs for some other kind of evil."

James stepped forward and gathered her into his arms to hold her close. Her body trembled in his arms and he held her tighter, wishing he could take away whatever fear she had experienced.

"Emma," he whispered against her hair. "I'm so sorry."

She shook her head as she drew away from him. Out of his arms, taking her warmth with her, leaving him cold as she stepped back, back and away from him.

"I'm—I'm fine," she said, metering her tone so that she no

longer showed him all her emotions. "He was drunk and angry and...driven to punish us both for breaking whatever promise my father made to him." Her hands shook and she balled them up at her sides. "Thank you for saving me."

"It is my job to save you," he said. "My greatest duty as your husband will be to protect you from all harm. I should have guessed Sir Archibald might be so foolish as to threaten you. I will never allow that to happen again, Emma. Once we are married I will ensure you are protected at all times."

He expected her to smile at that claim. Perhaps even return to his arms for a kiss. But her face remained taut with dark emotion and pale as paper. She dropped her chin, refusing to hold his gaze.

"James," she whispered, her voice breaking. "I-I appreciate your desire to protect me. I do. But something has become very clear to me today."

He wrinkled his brow. "Clear? And what is that?"

"I can't marry you, James. I-I don't want to."

The words Emma had just forced from her trembling lips were the most difficult she had ever said, made even more difficult by James's overwhelming presence in the tight space of the stable stall. He had swept in to rescue her, and it would be so easy to allow him to cradle and protect her forever.

But she wanted more than that. More from him. Not getting it would only result in ruin and despair in the future.

"Have you struck your head, Emma?" he asked at last, his tone filled with incredulity.

"Of course not."

"Then what in the world can you mean that you don't want to marry me?" he asked, his tone tense as a wire stretched to the breaking point.

The part of her that had always stood along the wall, the

part of her that had lived in fear from the time she was old enough to know her father could ruin her, wanted to apologize to James. To bend to his will and say she was mistaken and step into the future of his design.

But there was another part of her now. A part that recognized her own worth. Ironically, it was a part that James, himself, had helped her find. And this was the part that told her to walk away from him.

"I saw you," she said softly.

He swallowed hard. "Saw me?" he repeated.

She forced her gaze to lock with his and held there. "I saw you on the terrace. With Lady Montague."

She expected him to react with shock and then to deny her claim. That was what her father would have done. Hell, *had* done a dozen times or more, when her mother confronted him about his affairs over the years. Emma had witnessed those horrible rows. Her mother crying, her father offended at the accusations. Eventually her mother would capitulate. Eventually he would leave again.

It was a never-ending cycle.

Only James didn't look shocked by her accusation, only grim. And to her surprise, he nodded. "I thought you might have seen us. Grimble said you went out to the terrace to find me and left the house shortly thereafter."

She clenched her jaw. "I saw you talking. *Flirting.*"

He shook his head slowly, the denial she had been waiting for at last finding his lips. "I assure you, I was not flirting with Lady Montague."

Anger swelled in her, hurt and betrayal that she knew she didn't deserve to feel. James didn't love her. He had never vowed that he did, nor that he would be faithful. Most men of his ilk were not.

But she still wanted that from him, foolish as she was. At the least, she wanted honesty from him.

"I *saw* it," she repeated, her voice rising. "And I recognize it for what it is, James—don't pretend I'm a fool. I watched my father play those same games all my life."

"I am not your father," he said softly, but there was no gentleness in his tone.

"Well, I have no wish to be my mother," she snapped back. "Loving you and forgiving every lie you tell, like a fool."

"I'm not your father," he repeated, his tone harsher than even before. But then his face changed and he stared at her. "Did you just say you loved me?"

Emma's lips parted. In her upset, she had said those words. She had revealed herself. She was surprised to find she didn't regret that action. Now that it was out, she could explain better to him why she had to walk away.

"There are two parts to me, James," she began, shocked her voice was calm and steady. "There is the girl who always hid away, sat along a wall, tried not be noticed, especially by a man like you. And she is strong inside of me. She tells me to deny my heart, to protect myself by lying to you. Lying to me."

He moved toward her a fraction, and her hands began to shake. "And what is the other part?"

"The other part is stronger now," she whispered. "The other part doesn't want to live in shadows and with lies ever again. The other part tells me to confess the truth to you."

"And what is the truth?" he pushed.

She let out a sob and bent slightly as she struggled to catch her breath. Finally, she straightened back up.

"That I love you, you great oaf," she burst out, blushing at her directness. "Like a fool, I love you."

CHAPTER TWENTY-TWO

James could hardly breathe. The power of Emma's even stare, the power of her words, washed over him. Emma Liston loved him. She *loved* him.

A terrifying and wonderful concept that all at once made his head spin and his legs tremble.

And yet she didn't look pleased about that confession, nor did it change the fact that she had told him she didn't want to marry him.

"Why are you a fool to love me?" he asked softly. "Because I am not worthy of your love?"

Her lips parted and she reached for him, touching him for the first time since they'd begun this conversation. She caught one of his hands in both of hers and lifted it to her chest.

"Great God, no, James. That is your father talking, not me."

His heart lurched. "What do you know of my father?" he asked. She tilted her head and he shook his own. "Meg. She told you about him. About us?"

She nodded. "A little. But don't be angry with her. I asked, I pried."

"I'm...not," he said slowly, and realized it was true. Very few people knew about his relationship with his father. All of them were people he trusted to his core. Emma certainly fit that description. "If we are to marry, which is a topic we still have to discuss, then you have a right to know. My father was...cruel."

Emma sucked in a breath. "Meg said something similar."

"He'd lost his first son, his first wife. They were the family he really wanted." James fought the pain that accompanied those words. "We were a replacement. I never lived up to the original. I never earned the love he felt for his son. His *true* son."

She gripped his hand tighter. "You were a boy, you should not have had to earn anything. Love is not a bartering tool, James. That he used it as a reward rather than a gift says everything about him and nothing about you. You deserved more."

He looked down into her eyes and saw reflected there the life he would lead with her. A life of love and happiness, of protection, not just of him to her, but of her to him. He saw children and a chance to be the father he'd never had.

He saw his future, and in that moment he swelled with a desperation not to lose it. Not to lose her and the love she offered. The love he felt in return but had been hiding.

"Emma," he whispered. "Lady Montague approached me on the terrace and she wanted to be my mistress."

She made a soft sound of pain in the back of her throat that stabbed him in the heart, and moved to pull away from him. He clung to her hand, holding her in place.

"Listen," he said softly. "Please look at me and truly hear what I'm about to say."

Her breath came short, but she stopped struggling and looked at him with teary eyes. "Very well. What do you have to say?"

He swallowed hard. "I didn't want her," he said.

Her brow wrinkled. "But she is beautiful and popular, better matched to you than I would ever be. And everyone knows the rumors of her...her...experience. Many men take a lover and—"

"I don't care," he interrupted before she could waste any more breath on convincing him. "I don't *want* her. I didn't want her when she made the offer. And I told her so. I only want you."

She blinked, rapid little flutterings, like a bird struggling to take flight. "But you're…you. And I'm…me."

"You keep saying that," he said, frustrated by her continued self-deprecation. "But I've never thought that you didn't match me. In fact, this new side of you that you described earlier, the one that is willing to confront me, to walk away from me if you think I've betrayed you…that Emma may be far above me. I like her. I like the original Emma too. The bluestocking wallflower with all that passion hiding beneath her surface is exactly who I became enthralled with. I want *you*, Emma. All the parts and sides of you."

"You truly refused her?" she whispered.

He nodded slowly. "I did. And I will refuse any other offer I may get in the future. I'm not your father, Emma. I will never betray you as long as I have breath in my body."

She let out a shuddering sigh. "And I am not *your* father, James. I will never use love as a bargaining chip." She shook her head. "Aren't we a pair, though?"

"Yes," he said with a small laugh. "It seems we've both been so tangled up in the past, we were ready to let it ruin our future."

She caught her breath, her hands trembling even though she continued to hold his firmly. "Do we have to let it?"

"No," he whispered. "We could start over."

She cocked her head. "Start over?"

He slid his hand away from hers and held it out again, as if to meet her for the first time. "Hello, I'm James Rylon, Fifteenth Duke of Abernathe. And I love you, Emma Liston. If this moment is to be a fresh start, that is all you need to know."

Her face crumpled slightly and she stared at him in heartbreaking disbelief. "You—you love me?" she repeated.

"I do. And if you will lower yourself to marry me as we planned, I will endeavor for the rest of my life never to make you doubt that fact again. I will endeavor to show you that it is true every moment of every day for the rest of my life."

She let out a sob, but she was smiling. Then she took his hand and shook it gently. "Hello, I'm Emma Liston. And I love you James. And you are more than worthy of my love, no matter what some crusty old bastard of a duke told you."

He leaned in and cupped her cheeks, kissing her with all the passion and love and surrender he had found with her. And for the first time in a long time, years, decades, he felt at home. Because his home was with her. And that made it safe.

He drew back with a laugh. "I think we just made our wedding vows. Assuming you will still marry me."

"If you wish to," she said, tears streaming down her smiling face.

"I used to think not marrying, not carrying on his name, would be my best revenge against my father," he said softly as he gently wiped those tears away from her cheeks. "But living happily, removing myself from his shadow…I think that is a far better revenge."

"Then let us go be happy together," she whispered, taking his arm.

He guided her toward the stable doors with a laugh. "Happily ever after."

EPILOGUE

Three Months Later

There were those who had whispered that a wallflower like Emma Liston could never be a good Duchess of Abernathe. But even those cruel gossips were begging to be invited to the end of summer party at Falcon's Landing just three months after her marriage to the duke.

Emma had only invited those she actually liked. Now she stood on the landing that looked over the lawn and smiled down over the crowd that was gathered for tea. These were her friends, her family. The only one missing was her mother.

She sighed a little at the thought. They hadn't spoken since their row before the wedding, though she'd heard through friends of friends that her father had recently abandoned Mrs. Liston again. She shook her head at the thought. In a few days, she intended to reach out to her mother. Perhaps this time she could help her see that whatever was between her parents, it wasn't love.

And if she couldn't? Then she would not allow it to mar her happiness. And she *was* happy. She had never thought she would enjoy being a duchess, but James made every day an adventure and every night a passionate exploration.

As if conjured by her thoughts, she felt him wrap his arms around her from behind and press a kiss to her cheek as he drew her back against his strong, broad chest. She felt the ridge of his erection pressing into her backside, and laughed. It seemed she would have to take care of that before they joined their guests, and she thrilled at the idea.

"They are waiting for us," James said.

She ground back against him just a little and elicited a deep moan from him that made her smile. "Obviously they'll have to wait."

She expected him to draw her back into the parlor and take her, but instead he remained where he was, holding her close. She turned in his arms and looked up to find him smiling.

"What is that look for?" she asked as she leaned up to brush her lips against his.

"I'm happy, Emma," he said softly. "I was incomplete and never knew it. But you came along and now...now I'm whole."

A lump filled her throat at the sweet confession and the pure happiness on his face when he said it. "I feel the same way," she said. "And I...I have news that will make us more than complete."

"News?" he asked, tilting his head slightly. "What news is that?"

She caught his hand and drew it down, pressing it to her belly gently. "A baby," she said, watching for his reaction.

To her delight, his face lit up and he dropped his other hand to her stomach as he stared at her in shock. "A baby?"

She nodded. "Are you happy?"

"Happy?" he repeated with a loud laugh. "I'm over the moon, Emma. All my happiness, all my world...it starts and finishes with you. And I can think of no better gift than a child to complete this happy union."

He caught her in his arms then and kissed her, at first gently, but then more deeply and passionately. As he guided her back into the house, into a parlor where he would prove his love for her once again, she couldn't help but beam.

This was her life. One she might not have ever imagined, but made her happier than she ever thought she could be. And one she intended to celebrate with the man she loved.

Enjoy an exciting excerpt from *Her Favorite Duke,* out June 6th

Simon shut the terrace door behind himself, then sucked in a great gulp of cool air. Since his conversation with Christopher, he had felt this weight pressing down on him, crushing him. He hardly recalled the last twenty minutes. Hardly recalled the dances or his partners.

He didn't recall anything except for the pounding refrain that echoed in his head. *Margaret. Margaret. Margaret.*

He deserved to be called out for his obsession. He deserved to be abandoned. And yet he couldn't stop himself from thinking about her.

"I should leave," he murmured. "Go away for a few months or a few years."

He'd often thought that same thing, but he never followed through with the plan. Maybe it was time to finally do what was right. He bent his head and stared at his fingers, clenched against the stone wall of the terrace. He'd have to make a good excuse to go. He certainly couldn't tell Graham and James that he was desperately in love with Margaret.

He was still pondering that notion when he heard a faint sound echo from a darkened corner of the terrace. He turned, looking around as he did so. He was alone out here, or at least he'd thought he was. But now that he was attending, he heard more sounds. Sounds of…weeping.

He moved forward, toward he darkened part of the terrace that was away from the windows and doors, away from where anyone would find a person.

"Hello?" he called out as he stepped into the darkness and stopped, allowing his eyes to adjust now that light no longer filtered from the house. When they did, he gasped.

A woman sat at a table in the shadow of the house, her head resting down on her arms and she was crying.

He rushed toward her. "I say, are you all right?"

For the first time, the unknown lady seemed to recognize his presence. She jerked her head up, turned her face toward him and he screeched to a half.

"Meg?" he whispered.

She didn't rise, but just stared up at him, her eyes unreadable in the half-dark. "Of course it would be you," she said, her voice thick with tears before she set her head back down.

He should have walked away. He should have gone inside and found her brother or her fiancé and let one of them comfort her as was appropriate.

But Meg had always been his friend, as well as his obsession. And he wasn't about to walk away in her time of need.

He took a seat at the table, sliding it closer so that their legs brushed beneath the tabletop. Slowly, gently, he slid an arm around her shoulders and guided her toward him until she rested her cheek against his chest.

She let out a shuddering sigh and the feel of her moving against him shot through him, waking every nerve ending, forcing him to face how desperately he wanted and adored her.

"What is it?" he asked, shocked he could form words when he was so damned aware of her in his arms.

She lifted a trembling hand and rested it against his heart. Certainly, she could feel it pounding, even beneath all the layers of his clothing. He absolutely felt the pressure of each and every one of her slender fingers.

"It's nothing," she said, her tone a little calmer now. "I was just overwhelmed for a moment."

He looked down at her and caught a whiff of the honeysuckle fragrance of her hair. God how he loved that smell. He'd planted fourteen honeysuckle bushes around his estate in Crestwood five years ago just to have a tiny piece of her there with him.

"Did someone say something untoward to you?" he asked. "Because I'll go in there and-"

She tilted her face up toward his and his heart stopped. Her lips were three inches from his. Close enough that he could feel the faint stir of her breath against his mouth. Close enough that kissing her would be easy.

God how he wanted to kiss her. He wanted to do more than kiss her.

She swallowed, her eyes going a little wild as she gently extracted herself from his arms, stood and walked out of the dark and into the safety of the light from the house.

"No one said anything," she whispered, her voice barely carrying.

He should have thanked her for moving them back into safety. What he wanted to do instead was catch her by the velvet sash around her waist and draw her back into the corner of the house.

He got up and followed her.

"You and I have been...*friends*...for a long time," he choked out. "You know you can tell me anything."

She stared up at him and then her hand moved. He watched it as she lifted it and pressed in against his chest once more. Her fingers slid up and she brushed just the tips along his jaw. There was no breath between them, no space and in that moment, there were no lies.

He could see something he'd spent years convincing himself didn't exist. Meg wanted him.

She pulled her hand away with a soft sound in the back of

her throat and whispered, "I can't tell you *everything*, Simon."

"Meg," he ground out, moving to take her hand.

Before he could, the door opened behind them. Meg spun away, turning her back to him, her slender shoulders lifting and falling on panting breaths.

"Ah, there you two are."

Simon turned to smile as James stepped out onto the terrace with them. "James."

"We've been looking for you. Come inside, will you? We've an announcement."

Meg turned around and Simon caught his breath. She had composed herself to the point that no one would ever guess she had been weeping in the corner not five minutes before. She smiled brightly at her brother.

"Of course, James." As she passed Simon, she shot him a brief look. "Thank you for the-for the talk, Crestwood."

Other Books by Jess Michaels

THE 1797 CLUB
Her Favorite Duke (Coming June 2017)
The Broken Duke (Coming September 2017)
The Silent Duke (Coming November 2017)
The Duke of Nothing (Coming January 2018)
The Undercover Duke (Coming March 2018)
The Duke of Hearts (Coming May 2018)
The Duke Who Lied (Coming August 2018)
The Duke of Desire (Coming October 2018)
The Last Duke (Coming November 2018)

SEASONS

An Affair in Winter (Book 1)
A Spring Deception (Book 2)
One Summer of Surrender (Book 3)
Adored in Autumn (Book 4)

THE WICKED WOODLEYS

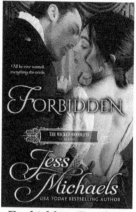

Forbidden (Book 1)
Deceived (Book 2)
Tempted (Book 3)
Ruined (Book 4)
Seduced (Book 5)

THE NOTORIOUS FLYNNS

The Other Duke (Book 1)
The Scoundrel's Lover (Book 2)
The Widow Wager (Book 3)
No Gentleman for Georgina (Book 4)
A Marquis for Mary (Book 5)

THE LADIES BOOK OF PLEASURES

A Matter of Sin
A Moment of Passion
A Measure of Deceit

THE PLEASURE WARS SERIES

Taken By the Duke
Pleasuring the Lady
Beauty and the Earl
Beautiful Distraction

About the Author

Jess Michaels writes erotic historical romance from her home in Tucson, AZ with her husband and one adorable kitty cat. She has written over 50 books, enjoys long walks in the desert and once wrestled a bear over a piece of pie. One of these things is a lie.

Jess loves to hear from fans! So please feel free to contact her in any of the following ways (or carrier pigeon):

www.AuthorJessMichaels.com

Email: Jess@AuthorJessMichaels.com
Twitter www.twitter.com/JessMichaelsbks
Facebook: www.facebook.com/JessMichaelsBks

Jess Michaels raffles a FREE Kindle or Amazon gift certificate EVERY month to members of her newsletter, so sign up on her website: http://www.authorjessmichaels.com/